MAGPIE

MICHAEL JAMES

Thought Catalog Books
Brooklyn, NY

THOUGHT CATALOG BOOKS

Copyright © 2015 by Michael James. All rights reserved.

Published by Thought Catalog Books, a division of The Thought & Expression Co., Williamsburg, Brooklyn. For general information and submissions: manuscripts@thoughtcatalog.com.

First edition, 2015
ISBN 978-0692596227
10 9 8 7 6 5 4 3 2 1

Founded in 2010, Thought Catalog is a website and imprint dedicated to your ideas and stories. We publish fiction and non-fiction from emerging and established writers across all genres.

Cover design by © Nick Kinling & Mark Kupasrimonkol

ONE

The birds peck and poke around the body of the dead magpie. They are looking for anything of value in the dirt and grime that coats their dead brother. There is nothing to be found and many birds soon fly off. Others stay – for whatever reason – and it is these magpies that I watch closely.

Looking at the dead magpie doesn't bother me all that much. It is the other poor birds around him that really get to me. I wonder if any of them feel anything while they watch one of their own cold and dead on the ground in front of them. I wonder what they think and if they even know the concept of death. The finality of it, I mean.

The wind lightly rustles the slick black feathers of the bird, as if gently trying to wake him so can fly again. He will never wake up and it makes me think of so many things.

It's always those the dead leave behind that can bother you if you think about them too much. Not the dead themselves, because they're already gone, and there's some sort of closure in that. The dead are often better off than those they leave behind.

I think of Saskatoon and my own dead magpie and wonder who will mourn him.

Magpies collect shiny things to decorate their nests. I read that somewhere. So now, when I watch them, I look for this.

Once, I saw a bunch of them fighting over a little strip of tinsel that had blown out of someone's garbage can. At first there were only two birds but soon more magpies arrived. This was good for there was no point if there wasn't an audience. Having bright shiny tinsel is useless if there is no one around to admire it. This is all that matters in a magpie's world.

One of the magpies grabbed the treasure in his beak. He puffed out his chest and called out to those watching. The other bird, the bird that lost out on the tinsel, flew off. I imagined him going back home to his empty nest. Once there, he will methodically tie a knot into a rope and hang himself. He won't leave a note because there is nothing left to say.

I look around my room. My own tinsel shines so brightly. It brings images of birds hanging themselves, or taking pills. All the ways a bird could do it. It doesn't really matter because magpies don't commit suicide.

The silence of this place is killing me. I stand up and walk out into the hallway where maybe I can hear some sound. Beneath me, the floorboards of this old house creak and groan and I like it so much I decide to walk a few times back and forth. The sounds of your house talking to you and only now you're finally able to understand it. It's been talking all along if you really think about it. Back when my mom was here, and my brother. The house telling us a story that no one took the time to hear.

I hear the jingling of keys in the front door.

Maybe it is my dad. He is home from work early because he finally snapped. He is only home to pack a bag before he hits the road as a fugitive. He is wanted for ten counts of murder. Our cells will be nowhere near each other but we won't mind. They have never been near each other.

I walk towards the door but before I even get half way there I know it isn't dad. It isn't anyone. All my edges are getting a little blurry. I can't tell what sounds are real and what exists only in my mind. My voice is real. This place is real. Sometimes there are other sounds and those aren't real at all. I hear doors closing. Conversations in another room that you can almost make out if you listen close enough. When you go see who it is, the room is empty. It has always been empty.

I look over at the clock on the microwave. It reads 10:23 am. This is how I know it isn't dad. He would never miss work for anything. Even if he did go and shoot up the place, he'd probably do it around closing time so at least he put a full day of work in. There are a lot of crazy people in the world, you know.

My old man is a strange guy. The way he slumps around the house you would think he got shit on by the world for a living instead of working at the town's auto body shop. Everyday is the same with him. He comes home around five, bottle of something in a brown bag tucked carefully in the crook of his arm. Usually whiskey. Sometimes rum. He pours himself a few stiff ones and sits down in front of the TV. He sits there getting good and drunk until he passes out around nine or ten. He pulls himself off the couch at around five in the morning and somehow makes it to work for another day. His ritual. Everyone has their own.

We never talk anymore. It used to bother me but not as much anymore. Some nights, when he's really drunk, he might get me to pour him a drink or find his lighter, but that's the extent of our conversations. I suppose I could sit with him a little more and try to talk or something but I never do.

Most nights I usually sneak myself a drink and go to my room. I guess this is my ritual. Every family has rituals, you know.

Sunlight creeps through the drapes in the living room. I wish it was the middle of the night and not 10:30 in the morning. I'm much better at night. You might like me a whole lot more if I met you at night and we got to talking a little.

One of my favorite things to do is get good and wasted and walk around town in the middle of the night. I pretend I'm dead and that the world is all black. I usually end up at the old elementary school. I walk around where I used to play when I was young. I pretend I'm a ghost and that all the kids are still there playing but I can't see them. I have an awesome memory and I remember most of the kid's names that I played with. Even the pricks that moved away. Anyway, I'll run around the playground shouting their names or maybe I'll take a little turn on the swings and have a deep conversation with one of my old buds. I know that sounds a little strange: A seventeen-year-old, drunk as hell, swinging and talking to no one. I'm just trying to be honest with you. Who wouldn't want to go back to when everything was normal and when everything made sense?

I think of the weed in the front pocket of my jeans.

The small bag weighs heavily in my pocket and in my mind and I want to get rid of it at once. I decide to flush it instead of dumping it in the garbage can. I always use to just throw it away in the nearest bin but once I saw some kids tip one over and I got thinking there was a chance that could happen again. They might go and tip the one with weed in it and find whatever it was that I had thrown away. I had to be more careful because you never know. Crazier stuff has happened.

In the bathroom I run the tap full blast. I splash water on to my face and try not to look at my own eyes in the mirror. The bag's contents disappear quickly and easily down the toilet leaving a slight scent that hangs in the air.

The smell of dad's work clothes on the bathroom floor mingles with the marijuana. Sweat and motor oil and the slight hint of whiskey. I pick them up and press them to my face. As a kid, I remember shoving my face into his work shirt when I would greet him at the door after work. It didn't smell bad back then even though it was the same smell. It just smelled the way it was supposed to. It is funny how something can stay the same but still be different. You change.

You have important work to do

I turn quickly towards the whispers but there is no one there. Creeping out of the bathroom, I cross the linoleum in the kitchen. I reach out and rest my finger on the blinds that cover the window above the sink.

Hey

I look for a man named Faran Bird and imagine him silently stalking through our yard. He doesn't exist in this place and there is no one out there.

The corners are already beginning to bend and stretch on my day. If I keep trying to go through it, and I keep trying to fix everything, I'm going to go crazy. I swear I'll go crazy.

The magpies are fighting again somewhere outside. I can hear them as clearly as if they are in the next room.

I decide to drown in their sounds for a while. The soundtrack of my haunting as I slowly move through this old house.

TWO

There is a drink in my hand and I squeeze it so that I know that it exists in the space outside of my mind.

I stand in front of the living room window, staring out at the world. Part of me is looking for the magpies again but they must have moved on. I think they have gone to see where the winner of the tinsel has showcased his treasure. Their envy is part of the prize.

The grass in our front yard is starting to die. It is probably just the weather, because it's that time of year, but it just doesn't feel right. It's starting to turn gray, like when someone fiddles around with the TV settings. Everything is not the colour it's supposed to be. It's not just our grass that's dying and there is a certain comfort in that.

I shut the drapes and decide there is no use staring at my dying grass all day. I will never save it.

What's he doing

I turn quickly towards the sound and a few drops of vodka splash from my glass and onto my shirt. The voice always comes from somewhere just beyond the edges so you're not quite sure if it's real or not.

I press my ear to the worn carpet of the living room. From here, I listen carefully as the house ripples and bends. There is nothing under the couch but I feel the space with my hand to be sure.

Next, I move down the hallway, certain I hear something rustling and moving in one of the rooms. One by one I check them and find nothing. In the space of the hallway I am as still as I can stand it while I listen.

The house hums and takes a long and drawn out breath. It's in this space that I hear something in my room. A quick thump and a strange sound I can't place.

I open my bedroom door and see my guitar lying on the floor. It had previously been propped up against the wall near my closet but now it is face down in front of me. I look at the scratches along its back and search for patterns within the grain.

My brother taught me to play guitar.

I decide I will pour myself some more vodka and play my guitar for a while. I can't play too long. I have important work to do. Eventually, I will have to figure out a way into the city.

I pick up the acoustic and feel the weight of it in my hands. As I turn it over I see that the top string is broken. The broken wire bends and curls against the neck of the instrument. I run my fingers over the worn frets and the place where the guitar string use to be. It could still play but it wouldn't sound right and I might be too fragile for that right now.

I toss the useless guitar onto my bed and think of places where I can find more strings. There are no more in the house. I've been breaking a lot lately.

I know Kelly will have guitar strings. I think I will end up there anyway so I will try to remember to ask him for some. Kelly is this fat asshole dropout I know. I think he's a few years older than me.

I guess we're friends.

His parents got divorced and now he lives in his grandmother's basement. We play guitar together once and while and sometimes I go over there for booze if I can't find any around here. I know he'll have some guitar strings but he'll probably want to talk or something stupid and I don't feel like talking.

Pricks always want to talk to you when you don't feel like talking.

I swallow the rest of my drink in three long gulps and walk back over to the window in the living room.

It looks cold outside and I think about my old army surplus coat that hangs on a hook near the back door. It's this ugly old green thing with Canadian military insignias all over it. It is about two sizes too big for me and looks tired and worn. I love wearing it because I'm sure everyone hates it. It's like saying 'I don't care' all day long and people don't like things like that.

I go back to the kitchen. In the cupboard above the fridge I grab the bottle of vodka. I pour a hefty amount of it into a plastic water bottle that sits patiently on the counter. I fill the rest of the bottle up with stale pop I take from the fridge.

When the vodka is back safely in the cupboard I glance at the clock. The numbers are starting to blur. It is 11:23.

I almost leave the house before I remember and run back to my room. I get these payments on account of everything that happened with my mom. It's not a lot of money but it is enough.

I pull out two-hundred bucks from my sock drawer and stuff it into my jeans. In my other pocket is a small piece of paper with a name on it in case things happen to go wrong.

I thrust my hand deeper into the drawer and feel for the cool metal of the gun. I bend over and the gun presses against my lower back where it is held safely in place by my jeans. I already have the weapon even if I don't remember ever taking it out. I'm not sure what kind it is. I don't know anything about guns. I've never even shot a handgun before. We used to shoot pellet guns as kids but nothing bigger than that.

It's a long walk to Kelly's house but I never mind the trek. I think it's because my small town still has gravel roads. There aren't too many left, but some. I like the sound of gravel as you disturb it. I remember being a kid and how my bike tires sound as they bounce along over the gravel. The quiet and constant crunching sound that follows you everywhere you go. It's too bad I didn't know that back then. Maybe I could have appreciated it more or something. Most of the roads are paved now. There is more and more pavement slowly eating up the gravel roads. Cold pavement that doesn't make any sound and leaves no memory. Whenever I walk around town I always make sure to walk along the gravel roads that are still here. Even when they're out of the way. When I walk on them, I sometimes pretend that I'm nine. I'm going over to my buddy's house because we're going to head out to the bushes and build a fort. I snuck my dad's hammer and I got both pockets of my jeans stuffed with nails. Buddy's old man has some spare wood so what we're going to do is load up his wagon and pull the spare wood out to the bushes. We have to be really careful where we decide to build the bastard because if you pick the wrong spot, and you start hammering away at the boards, the sound will carry a good mile. Then the other kids will come and smash your fort. We just finished smashing a few forts ourselves.

I'm crazy sometimes. I swear I am.

I hear his car long before I can see him. The deep rumbling of an old muscle car that will soon die. I make my way off the road and back onto the sidewalk as the car approaches from behind me. I thrust my hand into the deep pockets of my big army coat and pull the collar up until it rests near my ears. I glance over as the car passes and the driver, a kid named Steven, nods at me as he passes. I watch him drive off, his old car kicking up dust and gravel into a little dust cloud that swirls and dances.

I take a sip of my drink and keep walking.

Steven grew up a few doors down from us. He was two-years older than me but we were good friends as young kids. Back when we were all too young to care what we wore or what store it came from. There was no such thing as being cool back then. No one cared how much anyone's parents made or what they did for a living. We were all the same. We all just wanted to be happy and have fun because we didn't know any better.

Steven was pretty damn good at sports, even back then. I remember him bugging me to play catch or shoot pucks with him. Sometimes I would give in and play. I think he could see I was pretty awful and we'd usually stop and play something else. I would watch him out of my front window playing street hockey with the other kids. If he noticed me watching he'd sort of wave or nod, and then continue playing. He never came and asked if I wanted to play. Probably because he knew I didn't want to. I like to think that he didn't ask me because I was his friend that he didn't have to play sports with. We had our own friendship that was separate from any of that. I was his escape. As we grew older he played sports more and we hung out less. He wasn't like the rest of them. He wouldn't have made fun of you because you wore the same jeans every day and your hair was too long or that you were terrible at sports. He would never be like the rest of them. He'd be surrounded by his jock buddies in school and he'd still give me that little nod when he saw me. I wonder if he still ever wanted to escape once and while.

I keep walking. It is a while before I realize I can't hear anything. My town is a movie set. Empty cardboard houses with empty cardboard people. No one says anything at all.

I question if that really was Steven in the car. It looked like Steven but not how Steven should look today. When he nodded at me he looked like he did when we used to play. When we were kids. That was years ago though and he should have looked older.

I'm just tired. My mind is starting to play tricks on me. If I'm not careful, everything will bend and twist and break. It will be like broken glass. Jagged pieces I can't hang onto.

It couldn't have been Steven.

That Steven was gone.

THREE

I stand outside the side-door entrance to Kelly's house and take a few sips from my bottle. I try to remember how many times I have found myself here.

Sometimes I wish I was a smoker or something. You see, I always find myself standing outside of places because I have to work up the guts to go in anywhere on account of my nerves. The thing is that you can't just stand there. People don't like that. When you just stand outside, and you don't try to come in to where everyone is, people don't like that. I can't change that so I wish I was a smoker so at least I'd have a *reason* for standing outside. You can't just stand outside of places. You have to have a reason.

Mom taught me that.

I never knock when I go to Kelly's house. Once I'm up to it I just let myself in. He usually can't hear me anyway over music or one his stupid video games which he plays endlessly.

I push open the door and the strong smell of weed wafts out. I hear the sounds of machine gun fire and people screaming. All Kelly does is smoke weed and kill people. It really is like something out of *Reefer Madness*.

I walk down to Kelly's lair and pause, like I always do,

on the staircase. On the wall, about halfway down, is this picture of him that his Grandma must have hung up years ago. Kelly looks about four or five in it. He's got this sort of stupid grin on and it's the only way at all that he resembles the guy that lives downstairs. I wonder what the kid in the picture wanted to be when he grew up.

Kelly's body is growing out of an old and ratty couch. I can smell his odor from the doorway. He wears a wife-beater and his long black hair is pulled back into a sloppy ponytail. I don't think he has moved since the last time I have been here. I wonder if I was to come back in fifty damn years if he'd still be rotting in this place.

One of Kelly's friends is sitting on the other chair. His name is James or something. I have met him a few times and I guess I don't mind him. He doesn't talk too much which is probably why.

On the coffee table between them sits a pizza box and a small bag of weed.

"Man, you need a cell phone." Kelly tells me as I walk in and sit down beside him on the couch.

"Don't you guys ever turn on any lights around here," I say. "You don't have to sit in the dark all day. Why would anybody want to sit in the dark all day?"

Kelly ignores me. His pudgy little fingers click and click the stupid controller.

Click, boom.

Click, boom.

Click, boom, scream. Click, click, click.

It is enough to drive a person crazy. I am going out of my mind listening to it and I can start to feel my heart beating a little faster. I try not to think about it too much or I really will go crazy.

"You have to light them up with grenades before you

can send your guy in," James said to Kelly. I forgot how deep and stupid James' voice was is. I laugh out loud as he talks. He looks over at me for a second before turning back to his game.

They are playing some war game again. I don't know the name of it because I never play video games. I hate them. You basically are part of a platoon or something and you are given a mission, just like in a real life war. You run around and using ultra-realistic weaponry, you blow up everything and kill everyone. You can even choose what side to be on, which is really screwed up when you stop to think about it. Games like that should be illegal. Honestly, they should. Anybody that can just walk around and fire a gun like that at people without feeling anything should be locked up. You have to at least *feel* something when you do that.

"I'll tell you what's going on here," I said, pausing long enough to take another swig of vodka. "The military is using these games as recruiting tools. That's all they are. Pretty soon you won't have any feelings and all you'll know is which gun to use when you lose your mind. That's all you're getting from this. You might as well go and join the real military. At least you can see that you are shooting at real people then. They're all real people, you know. None of *this* is real. None of this is real at all."

I am too loud and James keeps looking over at me. I think I am making him pretty nervous or something.

"Relax," Kelly said. "It's just a game."

"You should have seen what I did the other day," I said, hoping to change the conversation before I completely lose my marbles. "I was walking home and Mr. Harris gave me the finger as he pulled out of the teacher's parking lot." Mr. Harris was the industrial arts teacher at school and he never gave me the finger. I doubt Mr. Harris even knew who I was.

"I was so pissed that I went home and filled a jerry can with gasoline. I poured about half of it into the big metal garbage bin behind the industrial arts lab and lit it on fire. You should have seen how tall the flames got on account of all the wood and paper in the bin. I was sure the whole damn school might have burned down the way the flames were going. I had to hide behind some bushes because a bunch of neighbors came running over and were trying to put out the fire before it got too big. I bet they weren't even worried about the school; they just didn't want their damn homes to burn up. That's the only reason that people do anything, you know. Nobody does anything at all unless it benefits them. In the end they put the fire out but I hope Mr. Harris hears about it. He might think twice about giving kids the finger. Who knows, if he does it again I might throw the gas and matches in the damn I.A. lab next time."

I am getting pretty drunk. I *know* I am getting pretty drunk because I always start lying. Only, it doesn't really *feel* like lying. It feels like stuff that could really happen if I wasn't careful. I thought Kelly and James would like something like that to happen so I told them it did.

"You talk a lot," James said as he continued to shoot people.

I think I better cool it a bit because I guess I am talking a lot. It feels like I have to. Every time I stop I get so nervous I think I am going to have a heart attack.

"How much have you drunk already?" Kelly asks, never moving his eyes off of the screen.

"Three-thousand dollars worth," I laugh.

As soon as I stop laughing I get so depressed I could

die. It feels like I can't even move I am so sad. I want to ask Kelly about his little brother because stories about his little brother always cheer me up. This kid was crazy. Not crazy in a bad way. Crazy in a fun kid way that everyone forgets how to be when they grow older.

"Hey, how's your brother?" I ask. "Seriously, how's he doing? That kid is a character. Anymore trouble with those Grade Six kids?"

Last time I saw him he was telling me all about how his buddies and him were having a war against the Grade Six kids at school. He was in Grade Four so they were up against some tough competition. They were throwing 'dirt bombs'- that's what he called them – at recess and the Grade Sixes were chasing them all over the playground trying to beat the shit out of any Grade Four kids they could catch. The way he told it you would think he was in World War Three or something. Anyway, he hadn't been caught himself but a few of his buddies had and it wasn't pretty. They would catch them and march them off like they were a bloody prisoner of war. They would line them up against the school wall and just pelt them with their own 'dirt bombs'. It sounded like so much fun I couldn't even imagine it. I would have given anything to be there throwing 'dirt bombs' with those Grade Four kids.

"Is he upstairs?" I ask. "I want to ask him about those Grade Sixes."

"What? No, he's probably at school."

"Do you know what ended up happening with the Grade Sixes?'

"What the hell are you talking about?"

I don't say anything. I just sit there and try to be quiet.

"How come you don't have a cell phone?" Kelly asks.

"I don't know. I don't want one. Why?"

"I wanted to get a hold of you yesterday. I got some more shit in and I want to know if you needed any. Pretty good stuff."

He always said everything was 'pretty good stuff.' It pisses me off.

"Is it from that guy in the city," I ask.

"What guy?

"Faran Bird," I say as calm as I can stand it. The name feels strange on my tongue.

"Yeah, I think so," Kelly says.

"Okay," I said. "I've got two-hundred bucks, that's it.

"What do you want?"

"Give me what you have for crack and the rest in meth." I always get as much meth as I can because meth is the worst and it shouldn't ever be on the streets.

Kelly stops the game and with great effort manages to pull his fat ass off of the couch. A deep indentation in the cushions makes me wonder again if he really hasn't moved since the last time I saw him.

He goes down the hallway to his bedroom and returns a few moments later, a shoe box tucked beneath his meaty arm. He puts the box down on the coffee table and resumes his position in the indentation.

"I don't know about this crystal though," he wheezes as he talks, winded from his short walk to his bedroom. "It looks different."

"Whatever," I say. I don't care. I was never going to smoke it. Nobody was.

He laid out two little baggies of crack cocaine on the table. The meth came in small, tightly wound plastic bags.

I put the money on the table and quickly stuff the drugs into my coat pocket. I take another drink from my bottle to complete my ritual. Everyone has rituals, you know.

I get up and make my way to the bathroom as Kelly and James resume their war. I can hear people starting to scream again as I shut the door. I turn on the tap to drown out the noise.

It smells like piss in the bathroom. The shower is dripping and the vanity mirror has a crack right down the middle so every time you look into it you have to choose a side.

It might be the booze or maybe the piss, but I feel like I'm going to throw up. I drop to my knees in front of the toilet as saliva floods my mouth. I see a lone hair, black and curly, stuck to the side of the toilet and it gives me all the incentive I need. I throw up over and over until my body is shaking and there is nothing left to do but lay there and dry heave. I slump to the floor and try to stop thinking.

You have important work to do

I lay there and take another small sip from my bottle. It is only about half gone and this brings relief to me like nothing else ever will. I reach into my pocket and retrieve the small plastic balls. I un-wrap the crack cocaine and quickly dump both of them into the toilet. It dissolves quickly in my puke. The crystals of meth take a little longer but soon they disappear as well. I flush the toilet two times, just to make sure.

I am a modern-day superhero. Saving the world, one crack rock at a time.

FOUR

Kelly and James continue to play their video game. They are smoking another joint and a thick cloud of smoke hangs above them.

I move into what passes as Kelly's kitchen. The tiny sink is full of dishes and a can of ravioli is open and rotting on the counter. "Do you have any beer in here? I shout.

"I don't know," Kelly answers slowly. "I think there's a couple in the fridge.

In his mini-fridge I find two cans of beer. I pop the top of one of them and drain half of it in about three gulps. The other can goes into my coat pocket.

"Is that coke any good?" Kelly asks.

"Yeah, pretty good stuff."

I am so bored with them that I can't even pretend any longer. To pass the time I start to pace up and down the small hallway. Up and down. Up and down. I am playing this little game with myself. When I get to one end of the hallway I take a swig of beer and try to name a celebrity that has killed themselves. Then, when I go to the other end of the hallway, I take another swig and try to name how they did it. It's just a stupid game. James keeps looking back at me every few seconds. I am making him uncomfortable.

Consider your brother

"What?" I yell into their lair.

"Sit down already," Kelly calls from his indentation. "Why do you always have to walk around so much?"

I don't think I can sit down in a million years I am so bored with them. I just want to go home. I am about to leave when I remember why I have come over in the first place.

"Do you have any guitar strings I can borrow?"

"I just re-strung mine yesterday," Kelly said. "Sorry bro."

I am too damn bored to be depressed about it.

My empty beer can is placed on the counter next to the rotting ravioli. I wonder if it will still be there the next time I am in this basement.

I wait until they are back playing their game before I quietly slip upstairs and let myself out. I always do this. I never say I'm leaving places, I just leave. It's just easier for me to be there one minute and gone the next. I think most people would prefer if everyone left that way. You see, no one is really ever very good at saying goodbye. No one I ever met, anyway.

I am half-way down the block before I realize that I never asked Kelly to say hello to his little brother for me. He probably wouldn't have done it anyway but he might have if I had only asked. It really starts to depress me the more I think about it. I keep thinking about how excited he was to tell me his damn war stories. He probably didn't have a lot of opportunity to talk about the things on his mind. His grandma was probably deaf or something and his asshole brother was too stoned. I might have really made his day by saying hello, I bet. Kids live for stuff like that, when older people take the time to say hello. I know I did.

Two boys walk out of the alley and I nearly run into them. They look to young for high school but it can be hard to tell sometimes. They wear skater shoes and tight jeans and slink when they move.

"Aren't you guys supposed to be in school?"

"What's that?" one of them says. He walks over to me, pulling his hands out of the front pockets of his blue jacket.

"I was wondering why you guys weren't in school?" I said.

Blue Jacket looks back at his friend and smirks. He turns his attention back to me and says, "I don't know. We're skipping class, I guess."

"Well, what are you going to do now?" I watch his thin face to see if he'll tell me the truth.

"I don't know," Blue Jacket says slowly. "Just go chill out somewhere."

"Do they intimidate you there," I speak softly and wish I had a cigarette so he might take me seriously. "Do they make you subordinate?"

His face is smooth and clear. He may not even be old enough to get acne. I wonder if he might be one of the Grade Six kids in the war.

"I'll tell you a little secret," I lean in close to him, resting my hand on his thin shoulder. "They don't want you to think. They want you to memorize. All the smart kids, the good kids, are the ones who don't think too much. They just memorize and repeat. If you think too much, you'll forget to memorize and then you'll fail their checks and balances. It's designed to fit you into the system."

Blue Jacket looks back at his buddy and smiles uncomfortably. He turns back to me and says, "Yeah, I guess."

"Are you guys going to go and do drugs or drink now?" I asked, searching his face again for truth.

"What? No. We don't do drugs, man," Blue Jacket shifts nervously from one foot to the other. "We'll probably just go play Madden or something."

"Yeah, but you *will*," I said. "You guys will do drugs and you'll drink because you can already see how they're lying to you. You won't be able to go through it all and you'll look for a way to escape."

"What are you talking about?"

I smile and it feels as though someone has frozen my face into this position. "I'm just bugging you," I say. "Everyone needs a break, right?"

"Yeah," Blue Jacket nods. "We want to be back for gym class. We're not skipping the *whole* day."

"That's good," I smile. "They have their ways to keep us there, don't they?"

"What?"

"I was just saying they design everything so we all fit in to the system. They want us to feel comfortable."

Blue Jacket doesn't say anything. Instead, he turns and joins his friend. Together they walk off and I can see them whispering back and forth to each other.

You have to be careful what you say to kids. They might not have the skills to sift through everything to make out what you're saying.

My brother used to tell me things I didn't understand. He'd come into my room late at night, after he had been out with his friends, and tell me things that had no place to go within my mind. Terrible things that have no choice but to sit and fester. As you get older, the veil slowly fades. You can't tell everyone all the horrible things crawling and scratching through your veil. You have to wait for all their veils to fade before anyone can hear you. Things scare you. They might be real, they might be make-believe, but if they both scare there's no difference.

That's how my brother could be a real asshole. He couldn't filter things into me slowly. He just dumped the whole pot of shit in and told me to sink or swim. Most of the time you couldn't tell if you were sinking or swimming. I still can't.

Those two kids skipping make me think about going over to the elementary school myself. I can go and see Kelly's brother in his simple and perfect world and part of me can stay there for a while. I know how to talk to kids.

I doubt that he would mind. He might even get a real kick out of showing off one of his older friends.

I can join the ranks of his army. Together, we could destroy the ideals that oppose us. I can walk through his world and exist in a space they may remember one day. Conquerors of the Grade Sixes.

I will run into one of my old teachers and we will have one of those stupid little chats about the old times and how much I've grown or something. I promise myself I'll just stop in for a quick visit, nothing more. Even if they beg me, I won't stay too long because I don't want them to think I had no damn place better to be. When you're my age you're not supposed to want to go back to your old elementary school *too* much because you're supposed to have better places to be. That's just the way things are.

I take a nice long sip from my bottle and start to make my way over to the school. I pretend I am a warrior returning from some far off land. I am coming back to my homeland to protect my people. They are waiting for me to save them because I am the only one who can. Killing whatever chased them through the rye.

My shoes are silent. They leave no sound on the pavement beneath me as I walk. The gravel is still and the memories I leave last only seconds.

FIVE

I will save myself a whole lot of time if I cut through the High School grounds.

Usually, I would have taken the long way, staying as far away as possible from the school, but I just want to get to where I am going as fast as I can.

It is raining now.

A light drizzle falls against my face. I run my dirty hands through my hair so I can see again.

I open the top of my bottle and hold it over my head so I can catch the rain as it falls. I can't really tell if I catch any. It all tastes the same to me.

This is the football field.

I am right underneath the goal posts. I look out at the field and watch as the rain falls hard on to the bright green grass. Last time I was here it had been raining too. I think that was last year or maybe the year before. I can't really remember.

My dad had a guy from work over to the house to look at a car. We don't get too many visitors so I had holed up in my room just waiting for the guy to leave. It felt strange to have someone else actually *in* the house. It was like he made it real by being there. It existed. My dad and me and everything else that went on in our house actually exists and other people could see us. I was hoping he wouldn't stay long but once I heard the sound of drinks being poured I knew it might be an extended visit.

I paced in my room until I couldn't stand it any longer. I threw on my coat and left the house quickly and quietly so that my dad and the guy never even knew I had left. I didn't know where I was going but I just couldn't stay there. I had to leave and come back when everything was normal again.

It was raining and I had no real place to go. I thought that maybe I could go down to the woods and build a fort for old time sake. Just like when I was a kid. Then I remembered that they were building a new sub-division right on the spot where we used to build. I didn't really care. I was too old to go and build forts anyway and even if I did it wouldn't be the same and it would just depress me.

In the distance I could hear cheering and shrill whistling and I remembered that there was a high school football game on that evening. I had never actually wanted to go to a football game but I was bored and sort of anxious so I thought I could walk over and hide in the sounds for a while.

Watch the magpies play in the rain

"Yes, I remember."

They cheer for the magpies

"It was the way their damn parents and grandparents were cheering and smiling and clapping their asses off for them."

What do you care about it?

"I don't care. It's just that they never knew what they were *really* like. After the games when they threw off their pads and fake smiles. The way they used to bet on which girl they could get drunk and sleep with or the way they used to taunt guys like me. No one ever saw those things.

It looked like most of the town was there that day. Parents, and grandparents, and all sorts of idiots crammed onto the bleachers. I wish I had the time to sit beside all of them and tell them a little story about whoever they had come to see that day. "Is that your boy there?" I'd say. "Oh yeah, he's a really beauty. Heard he slapped his girlfriend at a pit party a few weekends back. No big deal. He found some other girl to sleep with that night. What a terrific football player though, one of the best on the team. You must be so proud to show him off." I think I could probably find a story about every guy on the damn team. Even if I couldn't, I'd probably just make something up anyways just to piss them off.

I stood a few feet beside the bleachers so that no one could see me. I looked up at the clusters of fellow students as they huddled together trying to keep warm in the rain. The most popular magpies sat directly in the middle of this group. In turn, they were surrounded by the next most popular kids and so on and so on until the outer layer was filled by assholes thrilled out of their damn minds to be sitting so close to the only people that mattered. They laughed along at half-heard jokes and stories and hoped that everyone else from school could see them now. I didn't know their names and I doubt that the high school royalty did either. They were too cool for the losers and not cool enough for royalty. The 'nowhere' kids. All of them nothing more than a bunch of dirty magpies looking for tinsel.

It was raining pretty hard so I couldn't see the scoreboard at the far end of the field. We must have been winning the way the home crowd was carrying on but

I suppose you couldn't *really* tell from that. Kids from school went to these games because that was what they were *supposed* to do. Winning or losing wasn't really the point. I bet that most couldn't even tell you the score at the end of the game. Too busy talking, and drinking, and texting, with all of their idiot friends to notice.

Today the field and bleachers look strange with no one on them. It is as if the rain has come and wiped everything clean. I like it this way. It feels like I am wandering around in some secret place that I have no right to be in. I am a ghost again but instead of haunting my old playground, I am here. I look at the bleachers and feel everyone's eyes on me. They are watching me for the first time. In front of me a wall of football players run towards me. I hold the ball tightly in one hand. I'm running down the field with my eyes closed, feeling the rain and wind slam into my face. I hug the goal post at the far end of the field. I'm bent over, basically hyperventilating. I can smell vodka and for some reason it makes me want to puke again even though I have been drinking the stuff all damn day.

"You trying out for the football team or something?"

I look up. Scott Klassen is walking towards me. He has his back pack flung over one shoulder like he is as cool as shit.

"The way you're running around out there I thought that maybe you were going to go out for the football team." He wears this huge smile on his face as he speaks as if someone like me going out for the team would just about be the funniest thing since pissing your pants.

"No," I say between deep breaths. "I'm late for a meeting. I was trying to hurry, I guess."

Scott Klassen is a classic 'nowhere' kid. Of course, if you were to ask him, he would have told you he was probably going to be the school's bloody valedictorian or something. He was always walking around school with a huge smile on his face, talking with everyone and thinking he was their best friend or something. No one really pays any attention to him. I know because I watch for it. As a kid he had this really tight curly hair that would go all frizzy when he let it grow for a while. The other kids used to call him Q-Tip. I always wondered why he didn't just go and get a damn haircut so everyone would leave him alone. He was clueless, I guess. Anyway, in high school he kept it short so it was no big deal. The only other problem with the prick, besides talking too much, was that he had this sort of up-turned nose. You could hardly concentrate on anything he was saying because you were busy staring up his nose the whole time.

It bothers me when people make their own hell.

Scott walks over a little closer. He looks at my bottle and sort of puts his hand on the shoulder of my ugly old army coat. I bet he really hates it.

"Hey man, you doing okay?"

"I've never been so swell," I say, brushing his hand off of my coat. "I'm just a little late for my meeting. That's all." I take a quick sip from my bottle and smile with only my mouth.

"What kind of meeting?"

"Just a little thing a few of the teachers back at the old elementary school asked me to do. You know how it is. The classic little pep talk to the other kids."

Scott doesn't say anything. He stands there staring at me like a real prick.

"Hey," I say as sudden inspiration floods my mind. "Why don't you come with me? Seriously, we would have a blast." I push him playfully. "I'll even race you there and give you a chance to finally beat me."

"What do you mean?"

We had been somewhat buddies back in Grade Four. Nothing too close or anything but we used to play together at recess and sit in the library and talk about the Ninja Turtles when we were supposed to be reading or something. Simple kid stuff like that. Anyway, back in Grade Four, during the school's annual sports day, I beat him in the fifty-yard dash. I didn't win the race or anything, not even close, but I beat Scott and I remember him being pretty upset about the whole thing.

"You remember," I say and I playfully push him again. "Back in Grade Four in the fifty-yard dash when I beat you. You were pissed. Admit it."

"Grade Four? That was like eight years ago. Why would I remember something like that?"

He was acting like the race happened back in the bloody middle ages or something. It is sort of making me mad but I let it slide because I am hoping he might go with me over to the school. "You should come. Even just to walk around the playground or something. I'll tell you, there's this kid I know and he's in a hell of a battle with the Grade Sixes. He's only in Grade Four and all and…"

"Listen man, are you sure you're okay?"

"Why do you keep asking me that?"

"I don't know, you're standing out here in the rain rambling on about Grade Four and talking a mile a minute. You just don't seem right."

I turn and start walking towards the elementary school. Scott keeps on talking but suddenly I don't feel like talking so much. Pricks always want to talk to you when you don't feel like talking. They never want to talk when you do.

"Where are you going? Scott yells

"Nowhere," I say so politely it hurts.

SIX

I am walking down a back alley a few blocks from the elementary school. It's not a short cut. I only go this way because I don't want to run into too many people. I guess I am getting pretty wasted and I just don't think I can handle running into anymore idiots. I'm scared of what I might do. I just have to get to Saskatoon. That's all that really matters.

Every few feet I stop and check my bottle. It's almost empty. I'll probably have to run home after this for a top up. It would probably be best that I don't show up at the school with my bottle anyway. I'll shoot myself in the head if I spill some on a kid. I don't think I can handle that. Besides, one of the prick teachers probably would go and kick me out if they knew what was in it. They would never let me stay.

I tilt the bottle to my mouth and take a pretty healthy swig. When I walk into that school, I know it will be different but I still hope some of it will still be the same. They couldn't have changed *everything*. Even though people seem to love changing everything.

I keep walking down the alley. I peek in people's backyards to keep myself sane. People should pay more attention to their kids instead of their damn backyards.

You can tell the pricks that don't care about their kids. They were the yards with perfectly trimmed hedges and flower beds. There might be the odd toy out but you could tell that later on that night that kid's dad would make him pick it up because it was out of place or something.

Up ahead, perched on a fence, a magpie watches me. The whole town seems to be full of magpies today. Maybe it always has been but I just never noticed. I pick up a rock and throw it in the general direction of the bird. The rock hits the fence and the startled bird flies away. I watch it for as long as I can stand it. He is off to swallow a bottle of pills cause the futility of it all finally came to light.

I hear something carrying in the wind. It is barely there so I have to stop and close my eyes and really listen. It is the sound of all the kids playing at recess. The sound is so faint, so delicate and fragile that I feel afraid to breathe in case the wind carries it further away from me and I never hear it again. I sit there in this beautiful moment and feel like I am listening to my past. There's never really that many beautiful moments in someone's life, at least not mine, but this moment is perfect. I can hear them playing. They are shouting and yelling and screaming in that way that gets lost somewhere before puberty.

The school bell rings out and tears me from my nirvana. Shrill and drill like. I remember crying and hiding my eyes in my coat when the bell had first rung when I was in Kindergarten. It's really scary for those kids but soon you get used to it and eventually it doesn't bother you at all. Just like most things in life, I guess. I haven't heard that bell in a long time because I completely forget what it sounds like. I always forget the things that I wish I could remember forever and remember the things I wish I could bury so deep they never exist again. I wish I could steal that bell and take it home and ring it all damn day so I would never forget. You can't do that though because people will think you're crazy. They won't understand what you are doing and they'll just dismiss you as someone unstable. I'll never understand people.

I start running down the alley. It is too late and I am suddenly enveloped in thick black depression that drops into me hard and unrelenting. I was hoping to wander around and watch all of the kids at recess. I think it would have been so fun to see what kind of games they play now and what they like to do in their fifteen minutes of freedom. I will settle for even a glimpse of this heaven. I run hard. Harder than I did on the damn football field because this actually means something. I round the last corner of the alley and the school spreads out before me. It has this big green domed roof and for some reason it reminds me of watching the Wizard of Oz. We had this old VHS tape of the Wizard of Oz that my brother and I used to watch when mom had the energy to dig it out. The school is my Emerald City. There is no place like home. The wizard doesn't exist though. He never did. It's hard not to pay attention to all the things behind the curtain.

Almost all of the kids are already inside but on the far end, the younger grade end, I see a lone figure. He is dressed in a red and blue puffy jacket that looks like it was meant for minus thirty even though it was probably only minus one or two outside. I like that. This means that he has decent parents because they don't want their little kid to get even a *little* cold. I like that a lot. People always think kids can handle more than they really can.

The little person is twirling around and around as he makes his way towards the school. He is clearly more interested in playing all the made-up games in his head instead of going inside. I want to catch up to him and ask him what he is thinking about. I bet you no one ever asks him what he is thinking about, they just tell him what to think. I wouldn't harass him or anything, I just want to talk. I can tell he is a daydreamer like I used to be. I could sit and play by myself for hours. No one ever asked me what I was thinking about. A lot of things happen to a kid during the course of the day and that means there's a hell of a lot of things to think about. It's not like when you get older. Not like that at all. There's hardly anything new and the funny thing is *then* finally someone asks you what the hell you're thinking about.

Suddenly I don't want the kid to go inside anymore. I see the frailty in all of this. He doesn't know what will happen inside the Emerald City and what will happen when they finally force him to leave. If he knew, he'd turn around again and go back to play on the playground. He wouldn't have the heart to carry on.

How could he?

I start running again but I know it is too late. The little person was already at the doors of the school. He pauses for a moment, kicking the mud off of his boots. He is looking out towards me. I want so bad to know what he sees and what he thinks at this moment. I want to know if he sees me. Is it him or me that doesn't exist?

I stop running as soon as I see the red and blue jacket disappear inside the school. There is really no use in hurrying now. I should probably use the time to sober up a little before I go in this place. I mean, I'm not *that* drunk, but still. I'm a master at hiding it if comes down to it. When you drink as much as I do you sometimes even fool yourself into thinking you're sober. I remember this one crazy time last year where I could've won a Oscar. I had woken up at around two in the morning or so. I was coming off a heavy drinking weekend and sometimes when you're sleeping off a good piss up you can have really bad dreams. Anyway, I woke up in the middle of the night from a terrible dream. I won't go into it but it was pretty bad. About my brother again. My heart was pounding and I was so damn scared that I went to the kitchen and pretty much emptied a mickey of vodka into my belly. I just sat there all night in my room drinking my face off and writing songs no one will ever hear. In the morning, even though I was pissed out of my tree, I decided I better go to school. I went to every single class I had that day and nobody said a damn thing. Not one damn thing. I could barely see the chalkboard and all someone had to do was ask me a question and I would have been caught. Just one question about how I was doing and I would have been kicked out. Nobody asked me how I was. No one said anything at all. I should have been drunk everyday maybe.

I keep getting more and more depressed the closer I get to the school. I just want to see everyone at recess. I want to see all of the damn Grade Sixes but the playground is empty and quiet. Another recess come and gone like the thousands and thousands before it. I could always come again, on another recess on another day, but for some reason I don't think that was ever going to happen.

I decide I'll take a little walk on the sidewalk surrounding the school before I go in. I think it might give me a chance to sober up a little more. I wonder how many little faces are watching me from the tinted classroom windows as I walk. The school windows have some sort of special glass so you can't see through them if you're on the outside. You have to be actually in the classrooms to see anything at all. For all I know, there are kids in every single blacked out window I pass. I give a little smile to the blackness. Maybe no one is watching. Perhaps only one kid sees me. It doesn't really matter. That kid and me understand what I am doing and why I am here. If not today, then he will know when he is older. He will remember me and then he will know.

I smile at the little joke between us.

As I walk around the school I can't help but notice how perfect it was for a house. When I finally get around to making some money I promise myself I will buy this place. I won't change it either. I won't change a thing. It is pretty big though and it will probably cost me all the money I have just to get the damn keys for the place. I don't care. I'll slowly burn all the desks, and old papers, and class photos for heat. I could pile all that shit in the middle of the gym and keep a fire stoked so that it was just warm enough to keep me alive. I won't need it to be too warm anyway because I'll be wearing my ugly old army coat all day long. I'd never leave and it would piss all the neighbors off because they wouldn't know what the wizard was doing inside his Emerald City People go crazy when they can't figure out what someone is doing. I will sleep in the library and spend most my days reading all of the books I remember from my childhood and all the ones I have forgotten. When I start to run out of money I'll give a little concert in the gym. This, of course, would be the only time that anyone will ever be allowed inside. It will just be me and I will be happy.

I find myself around the back of the school. In the distance I see Mr. Letkeman, the school janitor. He is fucking with one of the water troughs on the back wall of the school. The troughs look dented and worn out. Kids had kicked them in again or hit them with a playground ball maybe. I bet that old bastard, Mr. Letkemen, has been fixing that same old water trough for thirty years or so. Right around the same time he went and lost the tinsel.

"Hey, Mr. Letkeman," I must have startled him because he drops his screwdriver. It falls to the concrete sidewalk and starts to roll toward me.

"Hello."

I pick up the screwdriver and hand it to him. "Damn kids again, right?"

Mr. Letkeman eyes me cautiously. "Can I help you?"

I smile. "Sorry, you probably don't remember me. I used to go this school a few years back." A lot of kids I went to school with used to bug old Mr. Letkeman pretty bad. Hit him with snowballs when he was out shoveling the walks or go and piss all over the boy's bathroom if they knew he'd be in later to clean it. Bug him about his grubby clothes. Kids are like that sometimes. People find it funny when people torment other people. I never had a problem with Mr. Letkeman. One time he found me crying in the bathroom and he didn't say anything to anyone. I thought that he would have went and told one of the teachers or something and that they would have come in and made me tell them everything but no one came. He let me be alone that day and I was always pretty thankful for that. Maybe he just didn't give a shit. Who really knows. People are funny.

"Yeah, I bet some kids can be a little stupid once in a while." I look at his clothes as I talk. They are dirty and worn out. Even his shoes have holes in them. I wonder what he had wanted to be when he was young.

"Oh, I don't know about that," he said. He chuckles

softly and I can tell he is a pretty good smoker. Probably die of lung cancer any year now. I am sure I will remember this little conversation when I go to his funeral. It's always the stupid little insignificant things that people remember about people that have died. Not the important things that the person would have wanted to be remembered for. Only the stupid things like how they sounded when they yawned or the way they smelled when you hadn't seen them in a while. Stuff like that.

"Listen, I got a few minutes, you need any help?" I wish I was a smoker right then. I sort of know he doesn't really need any help and that he probably just wants me to piss off. At least if I smoked I could offer him a cigarette. He might let me stay if I offered him a cigarette. We could just sit here and have a little smoke while we shot the shit. I would tell him how I envied him because he got to stay here. I sort of feel like a little kid, or something, just standing here without a fucking smoke or anything.

"No, I'm almost done anyway. You say you used to go here?"

"Yes. About five or six years ago, I guess. It was a pretty good school to me. It made me the man I am today. I'm getting ready to do my second tour in Afghanistan, that's why I'm here. They're talking about having me come in and show all the kids my war medals." I see him looking at my army coat and I figure he is probably interested in stuff like that.

Mr. Letkeman laughs softly again. "Your war medals?

"Sure," I say. "I don't talk about it much on account of the PTSD and all. They're trying to get me to start talking a bit. To help out all the kids, I guess." I probably actually had PTSD so it wasn't a total lie. What did it matter anyway, he was just a stupid janitor with holes in his shoes.

"You need me to show you inside?" He is looking at me in a funny sort of way now. It is making me nervous and I wish again I had a smoke, or at least a drink.

"No, I know my way around here pretty good. Thanks a lot though," I lean in and sort of pat him on the shoulder. As I lean in he breathes in deeply. He probably smells the booze coming off of me pretty good, I bet.

He wants to go inside and tell all the authorities about me. He wants to be the important magpie for the day. The hero for once instead of the dumb janitor.

What's he doing

I hear a voice coming from behind him. I look but no one is there. If Mr. Letkemen hears it, he ignores it as well.

I turn and go back the way I have come. I only have a bit of time left before the end of the school day and I don't want to waste it talking to some janitor.

SEVEN

It would be better for me to go into the school through the junior entrance. You are only supposed to go in those doors if you were in Grades One to Four but I don't think anyone will hassle me too much. No one will probably even notice me anyway, and if they do, they will think I am there for a good reason. People just don't go into a school for no damn good reason.

One must always have a reason.

I stand outside the doors and work up the nerve to go in. I pace up and down the sidewalk in front of the doors, running my hands along the cool black glass of the window. If only I had a smoke to hold in case anyone was watching. To be honest, I'm getting a little nervous and edgy. The alcohol is wearing off. I'm not sure I can go through with this and I can't remember why I am even here in the first place.

It is getting a little colder out and I thrust my hands into my pockets to keep them warm. My hands close around familiar smooth aluminum. It is the beer I swiped from Kelly's house. It's still cold against my palm and I grip it so hard it could burst. I resist the urge to pull it out and slam it back right there in front of the doors.

I grip the cold metal door handle and pull. A rush of

warm air blows into me and I breathe in deeply. The smell of paper and paints and the faintest trace of floor cleaner fills my soul. I recognize it instantly and it makes me so damn depressed. How could I could go and forget a smell like this? How could I come here so many days and forget how the damn place smells? I think about going back out and asking old man Letkeman what kind of floor cleaner he uses. I'll buy a bottle and use it to wash every damn wall and floor in my house. I'd just go on washing and washing until I wear the paint off the walls. I won't forget then.

I look over at the tiny boot rack that lines either side of the doors. Small boots and shoes waiting patiently for their impatient owners. They smell of sweat and water and dirt and I could stay here all day smelling them. Some were put nicely onto the rack while others look like they have been kicked off in the general direction of where they are supposed to go. Nothing has really changed and I am glad.

Once, when I was about six or seven, another kid accidentally wore my boots home. I had come out of my Grade One class a little late because I always came out a little late, and my rubber boots weren't on the rack. There was another pair on the rack that *looked* like mine, but they weren't. A lot of the other kid's boots were the same because most of our parents weren't going to go out and spend a whole bunch of money on damn boots that there kid was going to grow out of in three months, that's stupid. They would all buy the cheapest pair which meant most of us had the same boots and shoes every year. Anyway, I knew they weren't my rubber boots because my boots had a little number six on the sole. I had also taken a little marker and put my initials on the inside. The boots on the rack were size nine. I wore those big old size nine boots home that day, crying the whole way. I was sure my mom was going to be so angry with me for losing my boots. It was right around the time she was starting to go a little loopy anyway and this was just the sort of thing that would set her off. She never noticed. I got my boots back the next day at school and I don't think my mom ever found out.

The things a magpie will worry about.

Beside the boot rack is the washrooms. I quickly sneak into the boy's room. After I make sure the washroom is empty I open one of the stalls and step in. The floor is sticky and it smells like piss everywhere. I don't mind at all. This is what the boy's washroom is supposed to smell like. I pop the tab on the beer and take a few deep pulls on the can. It would be enough to take a little edge off and that's all a guy needs sometimes.

I am getting really depressed again. I keep looking at the little toilet and how it was made just for children. I have grown too big for it and it was no longer for me. I close my eyes and slowly sip at my beer until it is gone.

I suddenly remember Kelly's stupid brother. That's why I was here in the first place. Even though I might have missed him at recess I hope that maybe I might see him in the halls or something, or maybe run into one of his teachers.

I hold the empty beer can in my hand. I don't want to just go and throw it in the tiny little bathroom garbage that the kids use. That feels wrong. I reach up and sort of push at the tiles on the ceiling until they give away a little. I toss the can as far back as I can. Probably no one will find it until I do, when I buy this place.

I quickly leave the bathroom. I have no damn idea

where Kelly's brother's class is so I just start strolling down the hall. It's empty so I have plenty of time to look around and really remember the school. It really hasn't changed much. The only thing different was all the pictures and murals on the walls. I guess those have to change every year so it doesn't bother me too bad.

A bulletin board catches my eye. On the board I see twenty little pairs of paper hands that some class must have made. On one of the hands it has the kid's name and on the matching hand it had something they liked or something. I place my old hand on top of one of the tiny paper hands. His name is Luke. Luke's other hand said 'Rocket'. This kills me. What the hell did that mean? That's why I like it so much, I guess. Why would a kid go and like something as abstract as a rocket. A rocket to where? Maybe he was messing around with his teacher or something.

I laugh out loud and the sound is strange and flat in this place.

"Can I help you?" A man's voice calls out from behind me. He steps out from a classroom and into the hallway.

"Did you see this?" I ask. I was just looking at 'Luke Rocket' over here. Kids are so funny, don't you think? That's probably why you became a teacher in the first place, I'll bet? *You're* a teacher, right?"

"Yes, I'm a teacher, do you need any help?" He walks towards me and sort of rests his hand on my shoulder. "Let's go down to the principal's office and we can figure out the problem." This bothers me because he is a pretty young guy. Probably only a few years older than me. He's trying to act like some adult authority figure and to me he looks like a kid in one of my classes. I have more right to be here than he does, the way I see it.

"There's no problem," I say. "No problem at all. I was just having a good laugh about 'Luke Rocket'. That's all. I look down at his tie and notice there are tiny little hockey players emblazoned all over it. "Say, I bet the kids really like that tie you have."

Hang yourself

"You like hockey?" He is leading me down the hallway as he talks but trying to do it so I won't notice what he's doing. I'm not crazy, I just think the kids would have liked his tie is all. I'm playing with him, not the other way around.

"No, I don't like hockey, but listen, I do sort of need your help."

I tell him all about needing to talk to Kelly's little brother. I keep saying how important it was to me that I get to see him. I should be quiet and not tell him everything though. I always go on and talk too much and never keep my damn mouth shut about anything.

"Okay, we're just going to sit here for a second and figure out what's going on," the teacher said. "Do you know where you are?"

"Yeah, I'm at the damn White House. Of course, I know where I am. I only went to school here for eight bloody years, why would you go and ask me that?" I guess I must be yelling or something because he looks nervous. I'm not going to hurt him or anybody else. I just want to find Kelly's brother or at least walk down this hallway in peace. It's so hard to get some peace these days.

"Okay, just relax. We'll see what we can do about that."

He keeps looking down the hallway like he is waiting for someone more qualified to rescue him from this situation. I feel a little bad about this. "Listen, I'm sorry. I just had some bad news for the little guy is all. He's got this older brother and he's really overweight. He can't even get off the couch. Anyway, they had to rush him to the hospital. They think it was probably a massive heart attack."

He stares at me for several seconds. "Okay, let's go for a little walk and talk about this. Is that okay?" He kept saying that, like he was some sort of robot. They didn't teach him how to handle drunks like me in school.

Just go for a walk, a little fucking walk.

Just then I hear a door close softly behind us and the unmistakable sound of high heels on ceramic tile. Near the end, my mom *always* wore her damn high heels. She'd be sitting in the kitchen mixing up some scrambled eggs or whatever in nothing but her panties and her high heels. I know the sound of high heels very well. Sometimes, when I get bored, I go into the city to the mall and just sit and listen to all the high heels as they click and clack around the mall. I just like the sound. I'd probably wear a pair if people didn't think it was crazy or gay or something.

"Is everything okay here, Mr. Francetti?" The woman said as she walked up to us.

I recognize her immediately. Jenn Staley. She used to date my brother for a couple of months a few years back. Not too long ago, but long enough. She sort of looks the same but is maybe a little fatter. I see jewelry on her that sparkles and shines. Her hair is shorter too and I don't really like it. Why would she try to look worse? She recognizes me as well, I can tell. My brother dumped her because she was a no good high school magpie, I bet.

"Yes, I was just helping this gentleman to the office so we could discuss some problems he was having."

"Listen, I already told you. I just was coming to tell

the kid the bad news and maybe walk him home or something. No big deal. Why do you have to go and make such a big damn deal about it?" I feel a little embarrassed for yelling in front of Jenn. She probably thinks I'm a lunatic the way I'm yelling.

Jenn pulls the other teacher aside and says a few words I can't hear. I know they are talking about me so I don't see the reason why they need to whisper. If they are going to go and whisper about me then they might as well say it to my face. People never say anything to your face.

"Miss Staley here says she's going to talk with you. She should be able to help you."

"*Miss* Staley?" I smile. "You're not married yet? That's too bad. A real shame with you being such a nice girl. Did you know that my bro was thinking about popping the question to you himself? Seriously, he was."

I don't even think my brother even liked her that much the more I think about it but why be mean. Sometimes the nicest thing you can do is lie to someone.

"So you remember me?" Jenn smiles as she clicks and clacks towards me. "You were just a little guy back then. I'm surprised you remember that, Ben."

Man, I hate that. It was only a few years back. Why do people go and act like everything happened a thousand years ago?

"I'm sorry about your brother as well. I know how close you two were."

"Yeah, a real damn tragedy." I say.

I can tell she is trying to get me to walk with her down the hallway to the principal's office. I don't mind this time so I walk with her. I don't know what they are all so worried about. It wasn't like I'm carrying a back pack full of explosives and had a couple of guns in my hands.

Even if I did have that stuff I wouldn't go hurting anyone. Maybe myself, if I had no choice or something. No one else though. I just want to watch the kids play is all.

"So you're having a bad day?" she asks. She is trying to act all nonchalant about the whole situation but I could tell she is assessing me. I had enough experience with people *assessing* me to know what she was up to.

"No, I'm having a fine day. One of your students isn't though. I was trying to tell that to asshole back there but he wouldn't listen."

"Okay, just settle down. Everything's okay here."

I laugh out loud. "No it's not. The kid's brother is having a heart attack and I came here to talk with him." I tell her all about Kelly's brother and how it's really important that I speak with him.

She leads me into the office and has me sit down on one of the chairs facing the school secretary. I laugh again because I feel like I'm getting into trouble or something, like I was back in Grade Four and had to go see the principal. It's sort of fun in a way.

"I'm going to call the house and make sure everything's okay, alright? Jenn said. I can tell she actually believes me because she's sort of shaking, like she was scared or something.

"Okay, but you better hurry. I mean this is a serious deal here. I need to speak to the kid. I'm not sure there's anyone else that will be able to tell him but me."

Before I had walked into the office the secretary had been busily typing away. Now she has stopped her work and is staring at me. I don't recognize her, and she looked fairly young so I figure she is new.

"How are you doing?" I ask. "Welcome to my school."

"I'm fine," she replies. "How are you?"

"Not too bad. What are you typing up there? Important stuff I'll bet." We both know she is probably on Facebook or something. Being a stupid little magpie writing stupid little comments on her friend's profiles. No one likes to look like they're not doing something important though so I let it slide and don't say anything.

"Yes, just some school memos."

I realize that pretty soon Jenn was going to call Kelly's house and find out my whole story is bullshit. If it hadn't been her that had come out, I might have been okay. Why couldn't I just walk down the hallway and be left alone? What is the big deal?"

"Say listen," I say to the secretary. "I need your help a little bit. I need to know which class a certain kid is in. Can you do that? You could get that information for me, right? I stand up and sort of lean on her desk. I'm not being threatening or something, honestly, but I think she feels that I am. She pushes her chair back from her desk and is holding her hands up near her chest like I am going to reach out and hit her. People can be crazy sometimes.

"I...can't really...why don't we just wait for Miss Staley to come back. She should be back any time now."

I start to panic as I lose control of this situation. I start pacing up and down the office. "Can you help me or not?" I ask.

No one can help you

She stands and looks toward the back room where Jenn has gone.

"Okay, it's alright," I say, giving up. I'm breaking up around the edges and I need to get out of here. "Tell Jenn I'm sorry, okay?" Tell Jenn that my brother would have probably have married her."

"Oh...okay." The secretary mumbles.

I run out of the office and into the main foyer of the school. The hall is deserted both ways and I am thankful for this little stroke of luck. I know I don't have much time and that if I want to talk to Kelly's brother I had better hurry.

I run down into the senior end past the library and gymnasium. If I would have had more time I would have loved to have walked around in those places. Just to see if they have changed much. I would have loved just to sit in the library and read some stupid little books again. Maybe have a drink and a smoke and read some stupid little kid books. That would have made me pretty happy, I bet.

I worry that maybe Jenn hasn't called Kelly's house at all. Maybe she has called the police and they are on their way right now. I try to calculate how long it will take for them to get from the town dispatch office over to the school. They are on opposite ends of the town so I have at least a few minutes. All I will need is a few minutes. If they come and I am arrested, everything will be ruined. Who knows what will happen when the police get involved.

I run to the first classroom door I see and fling it open. I look around the classroom at all the little faces looking up at me. I see all the desks and the hand-made posters pinned to the wall. The sound of chalk against the chalkboard and the odor of permanent marker.

"Can I help you?" An older woman asks as she gets up from behind her large desk.

I look again at the faces and decide they all look too old to be Kelly's brother's class. "Sorry, wrong class," I say.

I run to the next door and the next, scanning the room for Kelly's brother or at least kids that look around the same age. None of the classes look right. In the next class I go into I startle the hell out of everyone. I guess I must have gone in a little too forcefully or something because I am so worked up. Everyone turns and stares at me and some kids even look scared. Like I was going to hurt them or something but I would never, ever hurt any of them. I see a banner on the bulletin board that reads 'Welcome to Grade Six'.

I smile as I look around the classroom. I wonder which of them were in the war with the Grade Fours. "Assholes," I quietly say as I close the door to the class. I don't mean it or anything. In my mind I am just helping out Kelly's brother and his friends, I guess.

I hear yelling behind me as I run down the hallway and I know my time is almost up. The other teachers start coming out into the hall and are busy talking to each other about what is happening. I can tell I am in some pretty good shit now. I mean, I know I shouldn't have just gone into every classroom like this but I'm just looking for Kelly's brother is all. It all makes sense in my mind and I don't think I'm doing anything *that* bad. In fact, I'm hoping the kids were all enjoying the hell out of it. Maybe they will talk about it at recess for months to come. I can't imagine anything better than this. It will be like I am a folk hero or something. Part of me will stay here.

I see the exit doors and run over to them as fast as I can. A red fire alarm sits about five-feet up the wall beside the door. I decide to give the kids one last thrill, and I pull it. The glass breaks and a piercing ring cuts through the air. I have always wanted to pull one of those. We all spend our lives aching to pull the emergency alarm and watch the glass shatter but we never do it.

I push on the door and run out into the school yard. All I wanted to do was watch a damn 'dirt war.' This is all. Everyone always goes and ruins things for everyone else.

EIGHT

I run back to the alley, certain that at any moment I am going to go and get tackled by some teacher. I keep looking back over my shoulder expecting to see a police car or something.

No one is chasing me.

I press up against the fence as I run like a drunken stealth ninja.

The fire alarm is still going off but instead of being excited by it, it makes me so depressed I can barely move my legs anymore. I must be crying because I can taste my tears as they run down my face. Everyone has gone and ruined it for me and now I will never again get a chance to go back. Not even to watch a recess because they will be keeping a watch out for me. I am not a danger. If only someone had taken the time to talk to me they would know this. No one ever takes the time to *really* talk to someone.

I must be more screwed up than I think because I had made a terrible mistake. I had run into the senior end of the school. This was for classes from Grade Five to Grade Eight. It was no wonder I couldn't find Kelly's brother. I just needed to relax a bit and I could have figured it out.

That's my problem. I can never relax enough to figure things out. That's all a guy needs sometimes, you know.

Benjamin, we've been talking and we're worried you're not ready to go back to school

"It's better than being at home where I'm all alone."

My voice sounds cold and metallic for some reason. Like it doesn't belong to me anymore.

I come out of the alley and cautiously look up and down the street. It is empty.

I run across and started heading up the sidewalk towards my house. I pull the hood up of my old army coat so I can hide my face. It wasn't too much further. I could get home and get a drink inside me so I could calm down. Then I could think my way out of this little mess.

I look up and see a magpie, maybe the *same* damn magpie, watching me from atop a street sign. He doesn't move and I'm not even sure if he's real because his feathers don't move in the wind and his beady black eyes never blink.

I think of reincarnation.

My head is heavy and I feel faint. I stop walking and sit down on someone's lawn. My mind is racing as much as my heart so I started thinking my little mantra inside my head as I sat there.

'One for sorrow,
Two for joy,
Three for a girl,
Four for a boy,
Five for silver,
Six for gold,
Seven for a secret
Never to be told.'

My mantra is just some old nursery rhyme, I think. Just

a stupid little thing I say to stop my mind from racing all over the damn place. A psychologist talked me into trying it. It doesn't work very well but it did allow me to say, "Yes, I use it all the time," to them when they would ask.

Expect destruction, connect with us

"Just shut up, what does that even mean?"

Sometimes these voices are relentless. They never stop and hardly make sense. I can't really make it all out so I try to talk over top of it. It's all a guy can do, sometimes.

I am still pretty anxious about capture. I pull myself up from off the grass and try my best to keep walking. I am only a block away from home. I could have a drink and be all right as soon as I get home. My legs feel like they are broken but still I keep walking. I pretend I have been wounded in the war and that I have to make it back to base before the enemy captures me. They will torture me for hours to find out what I was doing at the school. *My secret never to be told.* They won't believe the *real* reason why I was there. Not in a million years. I'll keep telling them and telling them and they will just continue to beat me until they get all of the answers they need for their neat little files on me.

I stumble up the driveway to our house and with shaking hands I fumble in my jeans for the damn door key. Why do I even bother locking it? I wouldn't have given two shits if someone had wanted to come in and take something. As long as they left the booze alone, they could have anything they want. What did it matter anyway? I don't have anything that I really need. I'm no hoarding magpie. I guess if people really thought about it they would all leave their doors open.

If you think you need it, I'll help you take it.

When I finally get into the house my heart starts fading

in and out of this place. Beating on this side and what lies beyond. It feels like it is going to stop beating on this side any moment, I am certain of it. I can feel it seizing and my throat has started to close. I run to the liquor cabinet above the fridge and grab the forty-ounce vodka. My hands are shaking so bad, and I can barely get the damn lid off. I bring the bottle to my lips and take a deep and long pull. I swallow three or four times before I take it away from my lips.

Everything fades away. I hear nothing but my own breathing.

I slump to the floor and lean my head up against the fridge. I hold the bottle tightly in my hands and just let myself cry. I guess it helps to calm me down. I will sit here crying and drinking for probably five minutes or so. That's all I need. Just a little bit of time to calm down and think. Isn't that all what we really need? Just one minute to think.

I hear a car drive by the house. I carefully place the bottle down on the floor and run to the window. It was just a plain car. It wasn't a police car or anything but it has me thinking that it easily could've been. Jenn would have told them my name back at the school and someone would have called the cops for sure. The first place they will come is to the house. You can't just go walking around a school. No one will understand that.

I pick up the bottle and start pacing again in the kitchen. Back and forth and back and forth I pace, trying to think of a plan. I take a quick drink every now and then so I can keep calming myself. I know damn well I can't stay at the house. I'd have to go *somewhere*?

I remember the time when my brother and I had got into a bit of trouble. Mom had told us to stop buggering around with her glass ornaments. She had these stupid little glass ballerina dancers that she kept on the mantel. There were four of them. They were probably only three or four inches tall. She loved them.

Anyway, my brother and I got to messing around in the living room one day. I think we were wrestling or something dumb like that. We got too close to the mantel and one of the stupid glass ballerina dancers fell and smashed all over the floor. We knew as soon as mom got home we'd have sore asses for a week. I remember we hid out in the garage behind the house. We knew we would get in trouble eventually but it seemed like a good idea at the time. I guess we just hid out there so that we wouldn't be in the house when she got home and saw the ballerina busted on the floor. That would have been a bad site. Mom was a little kooky about those ballerinas. She said they used to dance for her at night when no one was watching. She'd tell us all about how sad they were for their lost sister.

You don't know someone is crazy when you're a kid. That word doesn't really make sense to you and especially not if it's your mother. You just think that that's the way things are. There's no such thing as crazy to a little kid.

I think that I'll go back to the garage now. Just for a little bit. I'll have a few drinks and sit in the car and just think. No one would think to check for me in there. I bet if I really want, I could stay out there for days. As long as I had a little bit of booze and some food, maybe my guitar strings even, I could stay out there forever. I guess it was just like the damn ballerinas though. I couldn't hide out for too long. I just want a little time. I think everything will work out if I just have a little more time.

I go back to the front window and give the street a

quick scan. It's still quiet. I run back to my room and begin rummaging through my sock drawer. This is where I keep all of my money. I don't trust banks and I can't figure out why everyone else does. Just because I put my money into a bank doesn't mean it's a guaranteed thing that I can just go and get it all out again whenever I want it. I mean, obviously most of the time you can. It's not like they're *trying* to screw you. Most people don't think about it too often, but not all money is even real. Money just moves around electronically from account to account. It's all in credit cards and debit and all sorts of ways that people deal with imaginary money. If everyone went to the bank at the exact same time and demanded their money, the bank wouldn't have enough physical cash on hand to give it to them. It would have to go and be in imaginary money again. What's money anyway? Just a bunch of paper. It's not really *worth* anything. When I had some time I thought I would try to buy some gold. At least then it would be real. Then, when ever everything went and fell apart, I'd have a little real money left. Everyone else would starve, I guess, and eat all of their paper.

I think about stuff like that sometimes. The world falling apart.

I can't find anything in my drawer. All of it was spent at Kelly's house. I know the old man had some cash he kept in a little box in one of his dresser drawers. I don't know why he kept money there. Maybe he doesn't trust banks either. I hesitate a little before I take it but I don't think he'll notice. I would only be borrowing it for a little while anyway. I'll put it back as soon as another one of my damn checks came in again. I count out two-hundred dollars and stuff it into one of the pockets of my old army coat.

I take one last look out the front window. The streets are still empty. Maybe no one at the school has called the cops. They took it easy on one of their old alumni maybe. I can't take that chance though. I grab the cordless phone and head out the back door. My dad won't notice it was missing. It's wasn't like *he* was going to go and call someone. People from the school, or maybe even the cops, might try calling him though, after he got home from work. The phone will be safe with me.

NINE

I walk across the backyard with the bottle of vodka in one hand and the cordless phone in the other. Our garage sort of sits at the back of the yard so you actually have to drive down the back alley to park a car in it. The outside of the garage is in pretty rough shape. Even worse shape than the old house is in. The blue siding is all cracked and weather faded and half the bloody shingles on the roof blew off years ago. It doesn't really matter though. If it weren't for the car inside, the place could have fallen over yesterday and no one would have really cared. Good riddance almost, given everything that has happened. I just liked to come out there to chill out sometimes. Like my brother did. It was just a stupid little place where everyone could leave you alone.

I take another swig from the vodka bottle. The bottle was half empty or half full, depending on how a guy looked at it on a certain day. Maybe it would be enough for the rest of the day, but then again, maybe not. Some days I drink more than others. Depending on what kind of day it was or what I was thinking about. Sometimes I only needed a little. Other times, I could drink until I died.

The small garage smells of motor oil and gasoline and

stale old beer. The walls are mostly bare, the tools and other items from the shelves moved to the basement a year or so ago. Against the far wall there are about twenty cases of empty beer bottles. In front of the bottles are a few old empty paint cans and a couple of boxes of dirty rags. A single light bulb lights the room.

I set my vodka down onto the work counter and place the phone carefully beside it. I am trying to be cautious and deliberate with everything. I wouldn't want to go and drop the damn vodka now. Not when it was just starting to work. In fact, I am starting to feel pretty calm again. I have a nice little buzz going and I am sure I have a good hiding place. I can just sit in here and relax and think for a while.

After everything was set, I carefully pull the fabric cover off of the car. It's a 1967 Mustang. Midnight black with yellow racing stripes. My brother's old car. It's not in the greatest of shape and probably needs more than a few parts replaced, but my brother had loved it. He had worked in the body shop with my dad, saving every buck for months so he could buy the thing. My old man and him would come out here all the time and tinker with it until they got it running good. I know it still runs fairly decent too because I like to turn it on every once in a while. I come out here and drink or whatever and just sit in the front seat. I turn the ignition and just listen to it rumble a bit. I listen to the memory of it. I step on the gas and turn the wheel but it's not like I ever drive the damn thing. I just like to sit in the driver seat and listen to music. That's good enough for me.

I take a cleaning rag out from one of the boxes and begin to gently dust the car off. It's not like it needed it or anything, it's just something I want to do. My little ritual. Everyone has rituals, you know.

I open the driver side door and climb inside, making sure to brush off my damn army coat before I do. My brother would have hated me getting dust all over the white leather seats. I sit here for a moment and close my eyes. Imagining.

I get back out of the car and go over to the work counter. I hid the key in one of the drawers. I figure I could turn the car on and blast some tunes for a bit. Something to keep my mind off of things. I take another quick drink of vodka while I rummage through the drawer.

My brother only had enough money to install a tape deck in the car. It was pretty annoying because it's hard as shit to find music on cassette tapes anymore. I mean, I guess I could put a C.D. player in myself or something but I don't really know how to go and do anything like that. Besides, I don't want to go and change anything about it. Everything already goes and changes enough as it is without me buggering with things.

I can't imagine myself ever going and saving for something like a car. I just don't care about things like that. Once I get around to getting my license, I don't care what I drive. Sometimes I see magpies I know, maybe a few years older or whatever, just back from working the rigs and bombing around town in their ridiculous trucks with the stupid massive tires. They are all tinsel chasing idiots. I mean, you'd have to be stuck in a bloody ten-foot deep mud hole to ever go and need tires like that. Why would you need tires like that? I guess sports cars are stupid too. Who cares how fast you can go? Where are you going in such a big damn rush anyway? If I ever had a car, I imagine it will be sort of like my old army coat. Just something big and comfortable that nobody else will like. 'I don't care' all day long again. I just like this old Mustang because my brother had liked it, that's all. It could have been a bloody bathtub with wheels for all it really mattered.

I get back into the driver seat, being careful that I'm not dragging in any mud from my boots. I lean over and pop open the glove box. There is really nothing in here anymore. Four or five cassettes, a little bit of loose change, gum wrappers. That's about it. I had been hoping to find a pen.

I hit play and turn the volume up as loud as it will go. I close my eyes and lean back. Imagining again. The music hisses and crackles over the old speakers, filling the car with powerful sound that lightly rattles the windshield.

I'm not thinking again. I sit up and turn off the music. Someone might have heard. If the cops were out looking for me and happened to come to the house, they'd hear the music and come around out back to the garage. I guess a neighbor could have called to complain about the noise too. I didn't think of that at all.

I get out of the car and walk back over to the work counter. I wipe my palms on my jeans before I grab the bottle. I just take a little sip this time. I'm already drunk enough.

My brother's voice calls to me from behind the wheel.

"What are you doing here?" Again my words sound metallic and far away. I can't see his face because the light bulb above is shining on the windshield and I am so thankful for this.

"You know, little brother. Just out here having a smoke.

The question is why are *you* out here? You can't be out here if you don't have a reason."

"I know."

"Why don't we go to the office and we can talk about it."

"No, I don't think so.

I start doing laps up and down in front of the car while my brother hums a tune I can't quite place.

"I don't want you ever doing drugs, Ben. You understand that?"

"What are you doing here?" I'm certain my voice is coming from outside the garage.

"We broke the glass ballerina's, little buddy. I'm taking mom to go find some more. Come with us."

I look up at the car. I still can't see his face but I do see everything else and it makes me sick. Magpies, a dozen or so maybe. All jammed up in the backseat. Their wings are broken and they're trying to escape and the sound is enough to make me crazy. I close my eyes and listen and sure enough, their frenzied shrieks mimic the tune my brother is humming.

I can *hear* it. I swear I can.

I open my eyes and they're gone. Everyone is gone and I'm alone again in the garage.

I have to find somewhere else to go.

I walk back over to the work counter and pick up the phone. I think about calling Kelly. Maybe he could come over and get me. I don't even know if he has a car or if he could even drive. I try to remember if I have ever even seen him anyplace other than in his basement and I can't recall. Jenn or the cops would have called him about his supposed heart attack though. He might even be a little pissed at me because of that and tell them I was over at his house buying drugs or something. I couldn't call Kelly.

Everything depends on me getting to Saskatoon anyway, so that's where I need to go.

I could call Jason. Jason could drive. He is a year or so older than me and one of the worst magpies I ever met. Once, I overheard these kids saying that he was this big-time weed dealer and that always cracked me up. Almost anytime you hear anyone talking about a drug dealer in Saskatoon or around here, they're always described as a 'big-time' drug dealer. As if every idiot selling drugs was a damn millionaire or something. Most of them could make more money working a part-time job at a coffee shop. I mean, he sold weed or whatever, but he lives with his mom and dad and drives a damn 1991 hatchback. A regular Tony Montana

I guess Jason isn't *too* bad a guy though. He's nice but almost *too* nice. It's like he's always trying to get you to think he's the greatest guy in the world. People hate that. I have known him for years because everyone in a small town knows each other from way back. I had gone to his fifth birthday party. His mom had made a cake with money in it. You got your piece of cake and you could keep the bit of money that was in it. I remember taking my $1.25 home and thinking I was rich or something. My mom said it was dangerous and irresponsible to be putting money in cake though so that was the last time I ever saw a 'money cake'. Maybe I'll make myself one someday. Put about a thousand dollars in it too. You'd choke to death on quarters. Fuck you, Mom.

I'm pretty sure Jason goes to university so maybe he's not even home. I can't remember his damn number and that makes me realize how little I know the bastard. I take a little drink to calm down so I can think. I finally figure it out after two wrong numbers. He picks up on the first ring and I think he must have had the phone up his ass or something. I would never go and answer the phone on the first ring. People have to think you're doing something and that you're busy. You're too damn busy to answer the phone on the first ring. They won't respect you if they don't think you're busy. People love a busy magpie.

"I thought you might be over at the University," I say into the receiver.

"What?" He paused for a second. "Who is this?"

"Charles Manson," I reply, bringing my bottle to my mouth.

"Oh, *hey* man." He says it like I was his long-lost buddy from the war or something. He thought I had died on the beaches but really I had survived and was finally giving him a call after all these years.

"I wasn't sure if you'd be home. I thought you might be over at the University," I say again.

"No, my classes are only on Monday, Wednesday, and Friday. Remember? I told you that last time."

I don't remember. I don't even know what the date is.

"Oh yeah, sorry." I say. Listen, are you busy right now? Are you free just for a bit, maybe?"

"Why? You need me to bring over some stuff?"

"Yeah. I guess you could. Just bring about twenty bucks worth. Can you hurry? I mean, can you try to like come quick?" I am sweating for some reason even though the garage is pretty cold. My head is all itchy and I am having trouble concentrating.

"Are you looking to score hard, man?" He laughs.

"Oh yeah, can you bring something else? Can you bring me a twenty-six of vodka or gin or something? I'll make it worth your while. It will all be worth your while." I am trying hard to not sound desperate because I'm really not.

It's just that he's nineteen and all and has wheels. I like to keep a few people around that are legal age. It just makes everything easier.

"Um, yeah. I could do that," he quickly agrees. "It might take a little while though. My car is fucked. The alternator keeps…"

"You can't drive?" I cut him off.

"No. I can run though. It's not that far. Probably take me twenty minutes tops."

I think about canceling the whole thing. It's not like I want to hang out with the guy. I just need a ride.

"Hello?"

"Yeah, sorry I was just thinking about something," I say, scratching my head really hard. Maybe I have damn lice or something. From the school. Kids always have lice, the funny bastards. "Listen, forget the booze for now. We'll get it later. Just bring the weed or whatever and come over."

He doesn't answer me right away and I think he thinks I am playing a joke on him or something. "Are you okay?" He asks.

"Yeah, I'm fine. I just had a few drinks is all it really is." What did he care about it anyway?

"All right. I can't hang out though, I'm busy. I have a mid-term on Friday."

"That's fine," I say. I don't want to hang out with him anyway. I just need him for a while. He'd do anything for a few bucks and some attention, that's the kind of magpie he is. "Oh yeah, I almost forgot. I'm out in the garage behind the house. I need you to come down the alley, okay?

"Why? Fuck, you're weird sometimes."

"Just don't go down the front street and don't go to the

front door. Just bang on the garage door or something when you're here."

"Really? You're out *there?*"

"Yeah, what's wrong with that?"

"Nothing," he quickly replies."Just didn't think you'd want to, you know, be out there I guess."

"Yeah, just bang on the door lightly okay?" I repeat before I hang up the phone.

TEN

I'm really starting to get nervous as I wait for the prick. I'm thinking some really weird stuff. I think maybe the phone line might be tapped. After Jenn had called the cops, they tapped the house phone so that they could get a little more dirt on me before they make an actual arrest. They know about Faran Bird and the gun and everything. They agree with me but what can they do. They're the cops. They sometimes have to stop the good guy even when all the good guy wanted to do was stop the bad guy. Laws.

I start pacing around the car again and I decide, if everything works out, I was going to come back and put a damn window in this place. Then, if anything like this ever happened again, I could at least see what was going on out there. I'm going crazy cause I can't see what's going on outside. At least you can see through the bars in a birdcage. It's not like this at all.

I walk over to the work counter and put the bottle down. My vision keeps crossing and I have to put my hand on the wall to sort of stop the room from spinning.

"Do you even know how to shoot a gun?" He says again from somewhere behind me.

I don't know. How hard can it be? I don't have to think. I only have to do it.

I ignore him and think of Saskatoon. The streets play out in my head like a movie. Or maybe like a play. I try to remember the last time I have been to a movie.

If I hadn't been drinking I would drive the Mustang myself. I mean, I don't have a license or anything but I was already in shit anyway so whatever. I could easily make the drive into Saskatoon. Park it at the mall or something. I'd never drive it if I had been drinking though. Not in a million years. I'd rather drive it straight into a brick wall than drive drunk. It would be all right if I was alone, maybe. On a deserted road with no one around for a hundred miles or so. Maybe then, I guess. If there was a chance I could hurt anyone else though, it would never happen. I just wouldn't do it.

Three quick bangs on the garage door.

I have forgotten all about Jason and I almost lost it when he starts knocking. My heart is pounding so hard I think I'm going to pass out. I grab the hood of the car and go down on one knee.

Jason is calling my name and I can't catch my breath enough to answer back.

'One for sorrow,
Two for joy.'

"You in there, or what?" He calls out.

I breathe in deeply. "I'll be right there." I stand up and walk over to the garage door. I think for a brief second that it might be a set-up, that maybe the cops are just waiting for me to open the door. They wouldn't do that though. If they really want too, they'd just come right in and take me away. Media snapping pictures of the crazed lunatic who terrorized the school and me, pulling up the hood of my old army coat over my head as they lead me out.

"You alone?"

"Yeah."

I open the overhead door maybe three feet. I poke my head out and see his shoes so that I know he is alone. He has these really stupid shoes. They are dress type with this dumb sort of buckle thing over the laces. The toes were pointed so they looked like elf shoes or something. You could tell he thought they were the sharpest thing since knives. He's always rubbing them and making sure they weren't scuffed.

"What are you doing?" He asks.

"You have to climb under," I say. "I can't open it all the way because I don't want the neighbors knowing I'm in here."

"Whatever," he says as he bends over to climb in. I can tell he's pretty pissed about it because it might make his clothes dirty or something. Guys like Jason can't stand dirty clothes. Someone might not like him if his clothes are dirty. I don't like him because his clothes are clean.

I apologized for the whole door thing because that's just the sort of magpie I am. Fake apologies all around.

"Don't worry about it." Jason brushes off his jacket. He has this leather jacket that he wears almost every damn time I see him. It's a nice jacket though, I'll admit it. His parents bought it for him for Christmas last year I think. It wouldn't be too bad but he always has to wear it when he is selling drugs. Even in the summer, he'll get a call from someone looking for weed and he'll drive home to get his damn jacket. I don't know, maybe he thinks it made him look more legit or something. People do the strangest things when you let them.

"So how you doing, bud?" He said after he was done fixing his jacket. "Haven't seen you in a while."

"I'm good," I say quickly. "I'm doing really well."

"Man, you're pissed," he laughs. "Who were you partying with?"

"Just a couple of guys from Regina. You don't know them."

He is looking at the car now. Maybe he's just looking at his damn reflection in the window glass, I don't know. He's looking around the garage like it's a museum or something. Walking slowly around, looking at the counter and then back to the car and then to the walls. It's just like a museum to this guy and it's making me angry.

"Listen, did you bring that stuff?" I ask. I just want him to look at me instead of all over the damn garage.

"It's sort of creepy being in here, you know?" He replies. "I mean, no offence or anything, it's just fucked up a little because of everything. Your brother."

"Yeah." I'm crawling out of my skin and I think maybe just another quick drink will help. I brush past him and grab the vodka bottle. I take a little sip so he won't know I need it that bad.

Behind me, I hear him humming that song. The one my brother was humming with all the trapped magpies in the back seat.

I turn. "What did you say?"

"Nothing." He looks at me and he seems confused.

"That song. What were you humming just then? What song was that?

He laughs uncomfortably. "I wasn't humming anything. I didn't say a word."

"Oh. I just thought I heard you humming."

He keeps looking at me strangely and then says, "I'm

sorry, I shouldn't bring that stuff up about your bro and being out here and all." He opens his jacket and pulls out a little bag of bud. He tosses it on to the work counter.

I pull out a twenty and hand it to him. "I really appreciate it. I know how busy you are and everything." I say, stuffing the weed into the inside pocket of my coat. I'll get rid of it later.

"That's what I do," he laughs. He's wearing this big smile like he just made the drug deal of the century.

"It's just hard to find people you can rely on," I say. I'm really laying it on this guy. "Most guys are assholes. They say they'll do this for you or they'll do that for you, but they never do a damn thing. Not you though. Your word is good. You always do what you'll say you'll do." I tell him everything I know the magpie would love to hear. It is sort of true though. He's so damn worried about pleasing everybody that his word really is good. A rare thing.

He's looking at the car again. "So here's the old Mustang." He says, walking around the side and looking in the driver side window.

"Yeah," I say, taking another quick sip.

"That is so *fucked* up," he says it so quiet it is almost like a whisper.

"Listen, I got into university," I yell. I think he might like something like this.

"What?" He looks over at me.

"My counselor thought it would be better if I just went and wrote the stupid G.E.D. Said I was wasting my time there and that I'd be better off in some university some place. About time too. I couldn't stand to be there for a second longer. Bunch of immature pricks is all it is. The place is full of them. All they care about is their nice new clothes and how white their shoes are. Not enough tinsel and tinfoil in the world for those guys to fight over."

Jason is looking at me in a way I can't place again.

"I thought you were taking grade eleven classes," he replies softly. So softly it's sick. He doesn't say it like he thinks the whole thing is funny or anything though so I don't mind.

"Well yeah, I was. That's why I just skipped the whole damn thing and wrote the stupid G.E.D. I guess my score was pretty good because I got a couple calls from some schools already. It was like being stuck in fucking kindergarten with those guys, honestly."

"Really? That's good man. Good for you. Which schools?"

"Oh, just some ones out west. Close to home and everything. I'm taking the year off to work and save some money. I'll probably have to get my own place so I'll need a good year of saving. Really looking forward to the change."

"You mind if I smoke in here?" He asks suddenly.

"No, go ahead." I understand why. When you don't feel like talking it's easier just to take a puff or something. Even that slight pause in conversation while you light your cigarette is enough to let the other person know you're bored with them.

"Thanks," he said, pulling out a pack from his side pocket. He lights it in a second, blowing the smoke into the driver's side window of the Mustang.

"Hey, do you mind if I have one of those?" I ask.

"Yeah, sure. I would have offered but I didn't know you were smoking now."

"Well I don't really smoke or anything, I just have this buddy who's always bugging me for smokes. He's got real short term memory loss or something. Anyway, he's always hounding me for cigarettes so I thought I'd hang on to one so I'd have it next time he asks."

"Whatever." Jason replies, yanking out another cigarette and tossing it over to me. "Hey, can I score a drink?" He asks, motioning towards the vodka."

Without even thinking I reach over and grab the neck of the bottle. I am going to pass it over when I suddenly remember why I have called him over here in the first place. "Hold on a minute," I said carefully. "I have a little deal for you."

"What sort of deal?" He was looking at me funny, like I was playing another joke

"I need a ride to the city," I said quietly.

"I told you," he sighed. "My car is…"

"We can take this one," I said, pointing at the Mustang. "I'll pay you…it's just that…"

"I don't know, man," Jason sighs again and runs his hand through his gelled hair. "I'm pretty busy with school. I don't know if I can swing it."

"I'll pay you a hundred dollars," I say quickly. "I don't care if you drop me off at the city limits. I just have to get out of here as soon as possible."

"You're going to pay me a hundred dollars to drive you to the city limits." he said it like I was pulling his leg.

"Yeah, I'll pay you a hundred bucks," I say, reaching into my coat pocket for my wallet. I pull out five twenties and lay them on the hood of the car. "I know it's sort of weird, but you don't understand. I have important things to do in Saskatoon."

"And you want me to drive that?" Jason said, waving at the Mustang with his cigarette hand.

"I'd drive myself but I'm pretty wasted over here," I

laugh, hoping to lighten the mood a little. "Just a quick drive, buddy. It would mean the world to me and frankly, I don't trust anyone else with driving this," I patted the roof of the Mustang. "That's why I called you."

He's not going to take you
You have to make him take you

"I'm telling you I can't do it. I'm sorry. I would if I wasn't so busy."

"You're so *busy*," I laugh. "That's a stupid excuse and you know it."

"What are you talking about?"

I think of the gun for some reason. The cold metal of the barrel and the bullets inside. Guns don't kill people, bullets kill people.

"What the hell are you doing?" Jason shouts and it sounds like he's under water.

I don't remember pulling the gun out of my pocket or pants or wherever I must have put it but I do. I can hear it banging lightly against the side of the car as I sway back and forth to the humming.

"It's an emergency," I say calmly. As calmly as I can stand it.

"Are you threatening me?"

"No, not at all."

I realize I'm holding a gun right now and the poor bastard probably thinks I'm going to shoot him. I could never shoot another person, I think. I could shoot a magpie though. I could shoot a dirty little magpie through the head quite easily, I imagine.

I find myself in the passenger seat and Jason is beside me. He turns the key and the car comes back to life. It rumbles quietly in the garage like it's angry. Angry because we went and woke up it up when it had only planned on resting in peace.

We pull out of the garage because I have to go to Saskatoon and there's really not much I can do about that.

Maybe, if things had been different, I could have stayed. We all could have stayed. They would never be the same again and so I had to go to Saskatoon.

ELEVEN

It feels weird sitting in the passenger seat of the old Mustang again and I try to remember the last time I had actually sat here. I suppose it had been with my brother but I can't remember.

Music is playing quietly on the stereo. 'Don't Fear the Reaper' by Blue Oyster Cult plays through the speakers and I see this sort of strange look on Jason's face as he listens.

"You should turn it down a little," I say, turning the little knob for him. "I don't want any neighbors to know we're out here."

"Is that the song he was playing when…"

"I don't know," I say, cutting him off. I don't know why he was so damn interested in the whole thing anyway. It's not like he knew my brother or anything. It's not like he ever actually talked to him, or knew the things he used to think and talk about.

I listen carefully to the car to make sure everything sounds all right. The last thing I need is it breaking down in the middle of town or something. Everything seems okay. In fact, I think it sounds better than ever.

Beside me, Jason is crying. I can hear him breathing funny and he keeps wiping at his eyes.

"It's just a quick ride. Then you can go. I promise."

Jason steps on the gas and the engine growls a little heavier.

I take a little sip from the bottle. The vodka coats my throat and cuts off my air for a second. I cough violently. I fill my water bottle up and it looks just like water because I have no mix. My hands are unsteady. I pour and drip vodka all over my jeans and the seat. It's okay. I'm fine with this for now.

Jason keeps flinching like I'm going to reach over and hit him or shoot him or something.

"I'm sorry," I say. "I'm on edge, I guess. I told you, I just have to get out of this town and into Saskatoon."

"What did you do? Kill someone?" He asks as the streets from our childhood slowly move past our windows.

"No," I reply. "I never hurt anyone. It's not like I went and shot the mayor or something."

Once, in Grade Three, I had run for Junior President of the school. Me, and the other idiot candidates, had made up these dumb little speeches with these ridiculous promises, like pop in the water fountain and extra time added to recess, stuff like that. I didn't win or anything and looking back, I'm glad that I didn't because it would have meant a whole bunch of extra work for nothing. I was only running, I guess, because I wanted people to know who I was. I didn't want to go and change the school or anything. The more I thought about it, that's all it is in a real election too. Elections that people actually pay attention to. I bet that stupid mayor, who ever the hell he was, only ran because he needed people to know he existed. To care if someone ever shot him. To know that he mattered and that he was an important magpie. I bet his campaign promises were the equivalent of 'pop in the water fountain' too. Nothing really changes, I guess. That's why I would never run for something as stupid as mayor. Even if I did want to really change things, everybody would be sitting there thinking I was just another dick who wanted to be noticed, and I couldn't handle that. I'd spend all my time worrying about it that I'd never get any real work done.

Jason looks over at me again as he drives. "Where am I supposed to go? What do you need to do in the city?"

"I have to go see a man about a horse," I reply, laughing at my little joke.

"Okay, as long as I only have to get you into the city, right? That's all I have to do?"

"That's all you have to do." I repeat.

We start to drive towards the towns' exit. I sort of slide down in my seat a little so that anybody we pass can't get a good look at my face.

Taking a nice long gulping drink from the bottle, I hold the vodka in my mouth, swishing it back and forth like it's a mouthwash or something.

Jason looks over at me and I see him gag. "How do you drink it like that?"

"It's just like anything," I say, my head resting against the cool glass of the window. "You get used to it after a while. At first it hurts but then after a while, you hardly notice it anymore."

"Where should I drop you off?"

"What?" I ask. I am beginning to pass out and I keep losing my train of thought.

"In the city, where should I drop you off?" Jason said again.

"I don't know," I mumble. "In the city."

Jason sighs. It's really annoying talking to drunk people. "I *know* in the city, but where? Do you hear me?"

"Maybe downtown," I say, sitting up for a second so that I don't fall asleep. "Downtown would be perfect so I won't have far to walk."

Jason is still crying but he's trying not to. I can tell.

"So what are you going to take?" He says carefully.

"What do you mean?"

"In university. What are you going to major in?" He was definitely scared and I think he's just trying to have a normal conversation so that he feels better or something.

"I don't know. History, I guess." That's what I would major in if I ever went to some stupid university for real. Hopefully it would be a big class with something like three-hundred students. I could see myself actually going to class then. I wouldn't know anyone so I could just sit and have a few drinks and listen to the lecture. It wouldn't be like going to school in town where I was constantly getting distracted by all of the idiots. I always spent most of my classes looking around at all of the other students. I had grown up with most of the bastards and because of this, I'd find myself thinking about them and how they used to be. I always remember things they said and did and I wonder if they even remembered what it was like when we were all younger. I don't think there is a single person who remembers things like I do. That's because I'm a realist, I guess, and I know things aren't going to get better. Maybe they would all take the time to remember more if they realized that back then was the best part of our lives. Everyone thinks they're destined for some great thing so they spend their whole life saying, "what's next?" They never take the time to look back. We're not special and there's nothing great waiting for us. They've left everything great behind them in their mad search for purpose ahead. I feel sorry for them all.

Stupid fucking magpies

"What year is this car?" Jason suddenly asks, running his hand along the smooth leather of the dashboard. "I like it."

"1967," I answer. I know he doesn't like the car and was only saying it because he feels bad about my brother and me and all. To everybody, other than me and maybe my dad, this car was a piece of shit, and I know that. It's not nice but that wasn't the point. It doesn't matter at all what it looks like. It's what it means. If it had been perfect, my brother and dad would never have worked on it together. All those conversations they shared, while covered in grease and oil, bent over the hood of this vehicle, would never have happened. If it had been perfect, my brother would have lost interest in it quickly because there wouldn't be any challenge to it. He would never have worn that proud look on his face when he finally did pull it out of the garage for the first time. So in a way, it was perfect and always had been. It's just that most people couldn't see that it was perfect because they couldn't be bothered to look hard enough. I'll probably have to look my whole damn life to find my 1967 Mustang, I bet.

"I'm thinking of getting a new car," Jason said. "An SUV probably."

"Just like a real gangster," I laugh. Jason laughs nervously too because he doesn't realize I am laughing at him.

"You mean it that you're really going to let me go?" He keeps swallowing and looking down at my hands.

I don't say anything. Instead, I lay my head against the

cool glass of the window and close my eyes. I can feel every bump in the road and it's making me pretty dizzy. I open my eyes and watch as our car finally exits town and we pull onto the cold grey pavement of the highway.

"Are you okay?" I hear Jason ask from somewhere far away.

Are you

"I mean, you *know* you're not okay," I tell Jason because I can't believe he thinks I'm the one who can't see things right.

"What? What do you mean?"

"Why do you sell drugs?" I ask suddenly. "I mean, for what purpose?"

"To make money," he says.

"Bullshit," I laugh. I'm drunk and I feel like I can say anything to this magpie that I want. "It's not about the money because I know you barely make any. I'm not some stupid fourteen-year-old punk you sell weed to, okay. I *know* it's not about the money. If it was just about the money, you'd quit school and have a job."

"Okay, it's about the *easy* money then."

"You're a liar." I shout into his ear. I'm angry but only because he thinks I'm that stupid.

"Settle down, you're loaded and I'm not trying to piss you off."

"So what if I am," I say. My hand squeezes the handle of the gun. I glare at him and in the moment I want to grab the steering wheel and jerk it hard so that we roll and smash all over the highway. "It doesn't change a damn thing with what I'm saying. I could be sober as a bird right now and I'd still be saying the same damn thing."

"Okay," he says. I can see him trying to look over at me

and still keep his eyes on the road. He looks so scared and I feel bad. "Just...settle down."

"You sell drugs because you think that other people will respect you and think you're cool and dangerous," I say. "Admit it to me. You want everyone to think you're a man now and not that little baby that puked all over the library in Grade Three."

"What? How do you even remember shit like that?"

"Admit it to me."

"I...there's nothing to admit. I don't know what you're talking about."

"Yeah, I guess not," I say. Maybe he really has no clue.

I turn and rest my head against the window again. I don't feel much like talking anymore and neither does he. We just ride along in silence somewhere along the highway between our town and Saskatoon.

TWELVE

Once, from the backseat of my dad's car, I watched a homeless drunk crawling down a street in Saskatoon. A bunch of kids, probably no more than ten-years-old, were following behind him. They were tossing garbage at him. One of the kids worked up enough courage to actually go up and kick the drunk right in the ass. They ran away laughing and the drunk was too loaded to do anything about it. He was nothing to them. Less than human.

I wasn't mad or anything because you never really know the real reason why a person goes and does something. Maybe the kid who kicked the drunk had an old man that drank too much and the kid was just taking out his frustration on him. Who knows the games going on in a young person's head? Sure, maybe the kid was just an asshole, but maybe once you heard the *real* story, you'd help him kick the drunk too.

I hope everyone knows my true intentions when I get to Saskatoon.

"You still with me?" Jason said, nudging my arm as we pass the city limits sign.

"Yes. I just need a moment to think."

Jason drives down Idylwyld. It is busy so I figure it must be rush hour. Maybe five or six o'clock. I think again, for probably the hundredth time, about getting a watch. I don't know why I don't wear one. I've even bought a few over the years but I would only ever wear them for maybe a few weeks at most. I always find myself staring at the numbers all day long. Almost like one of those obsessive compulsive bastards you see on a reality show or something. I mean, it was getting to the point where I'd be staring at the hours and the minutes and the seconds just ticking away and I couldn't do anything else. It kind of freaked me out a little and made me pretty depressed so I stopped wearing them.

"Where downtown should I drop you off?" Jason said, stopping the Mustang at a red light on 33rd and Idylwyld.

"I don't know," I whisper. I am getting pretty depressed all of a sudden. I don't want to be in this car, with this prick, in the middle of downtown Saskatoon. Take me home to bed. A large bottle of vodka beside me. It is too late for that, I guess. I am already here and at least, for the night, I am safe and won't have to deal with all that elementary school stuff.

Plus, I have to kill someone and set things right. It's too late for anything else.

"How about on Second Avenue." Jason suggests. "Is that close to your buddy?"

"What buddy?" I mumble.

"You told me you were going to see a buddy." He keeps looking over at me and nudging me every few seconds. He's so anxious to leave and now that I'm here I don't care if he does.

"Yeah, drop me off at the university instead?" I say, tilting my water bottle towards my mouth."I have to go and check some things out there."

Jason hesitates, and I can see his grip tightening on

the steering wheel. "Okay," he says carefully. "That's only down the University Bridge. Can I go after that?"

I ignore his question and say, "Listen, how are you doing in school?"

"In what way are you asking?"

"I mean in your business classes or whatever. How's it going with them? You always did well in high school but everything's probably different now. What are those business classes called again?

"Commerce"

"Yeah, in those classes. I was thinking that's what I might get into. Go through that so I can spend my days with decent, mature people for once. People in suits and stuff. No more idiots with skater shoes on everywhere I look."

"You just said you were thinking about being a History major."

"Well, I think about a lot of things. I have a whole damn year to decide, you know. Hell, you talk to me in a week and I'm liable to tell you I've decided to fuck it all and go live under Broadway Bridge or something."

Jason doesn't say anything as he maneuvered the car down busy Second Avenue. We pass a lounge I have always wanted to go into. It's sort of a fancier place, at least fancy for Saskatoon, and I have always been too intimidated to go in there. I don't know what attracts me to it because I know damn well it will be full of cawing magpies. I feel like I am drunk enough to stop in for a few so I ask Jason if he wants to go.

"At Baccus?" He says. "I don't think we should. You're pissed. You'd get kicked out before you could even order another drink."

"Is it because of what I'm wearing?" I say aggressively.

"Nothing is wrong with what you're wearing, alright. I'm not trying to piss you off again. What you're wearing suits you just fine."

"You think I should go and buy a jacket like you?" I say, looking over at the black sheen of the leather. I want to cut it a little right then. Not destroy it or anything but maybe make a little cut on it so he would still wear it but so wouldn't think it was so damn perfect anymore.

"Sure," he said, looking over at my old army coat. "You have money. Why do you always wear that coat? Go buy a new one."

"Maybe I'll ask my mom and dad to buy me one for Christmas," I say coldly. I squeeze the handle of the gun and hold it so he can see it. I swear I'd never shoot him and I mean it.

"What did I do to you?" Jason has tears in his eyes. "I'm constantly sticking up for you and telling everyone that you're a good guy, but you're not. You're an asshole."

"I didn't ask you to stick up for me," I yell, stopping long enough to take a deep drink. "Tell everyone I'm an asshole. Everyone that already knows me and everyone that doesn't."

I know he is right but I can't help it. Every time he speaks, I want to hit him. "I'm sorry," I say. "Listen, do you want to stop somewhere else for a drink? Any place will do. It doesn't have to be Baccus."

"I just want to go home," he sobs.

"What's that place called?

"What place?" Jason asks.

"That university bar, what's the name of that place?"

"Louis."

"Yeah, let's go there. Just a quick one. They get all types in there, I bet. They wouldn't mind my coat."

"You would...you would need I.D."

"They wouldn't check, would they? We'd be alright in there."

"No, we wouldn't. They always check at a campus bar."

We start down the University Bridge and I notice again how busy the streets are. I wonder how many people would die if the bridge suddenly collapsed and we all fell into the river and how long it would take before the newspapers stopped mentioned it. I imagine myself swimming through the frigid water, pulling people from their cars. Too busy saving people to come up for air until it was too late and I drowned. A hero. My body washing away down the same river my mother drowned in.

"You have to be careful around campus," Jason says as we exit the bridge and continue up University Drive. "They have those rent-a-cop university police everywhere and they'll see that you're pissed from a mile away."

"I'm not that bad," I reply. "I'm not planning on sitting and having a bloody conversation with anyone anyway."

"I'd be careful so you don't get hurt. They're going to notice you. People aren't stupid."

"Everyone is stupid," I laugh. "They're just too stupid to know it."

"Yeah, maybe," Jason says quietly.

Jason pulls the car over to a side street directly across from campus and little way down from Royal University Hospital. He lets the car idle for a while and I take the opportunity to check myself out in the console mirror. I don't look very well today.

"Can I leave now? I'll just get out of the car and walk away."

"Is that that old school house," I say, pointing behind

us at a small stone structure in the middle of a large park-like field. It looks small and out of place surrounded by the large buildings that mark the beginning of the University of Saskatchewan campus.

"Yeah, the Old Stone School House," he said. "Listen, about the car, I..."

"Imagine going to school in that place," I laugh. "Trapped all day in a one room school house, watching that stupid teacher try to teach all the grades at once, that's how they used to do it, you know. All the grades in the same classroom. What did you call it again?

Jason sighs. "The Old Stone School House."

"Yeah, it would be like you were in all the grades at once, in a way. You would be working on your own assignments but sure as shit you couldn't help but hear the other grades and their work. It would drive a guy crazy, I bet. Hearing the same lesson year after year after year. Yet, it would be sort of nice too. Make you remember how far you've come and all."

"Please, let me go," Jason says suddenly. "I won't say anything."

"Don't leave," I plead. "It'll be fun. We'll go fuck around on campus for a while. Have a few drinks and talk."

"I just want to go home," Jason whispers to me.

I see tears falling down his face and I realize my gun is still pointing towards him. I'm not going to shoot him. I promise I don't want to shoot him.

"Please," Jason said. His hand trembles as he rests it on the door handle.

I sit there in the car for what feels like an hour but is probably only a few seconds. "Do you have enough money for a cab?"

"I have that money from the weed I sold you."

I can hear the humming again. The tune I can almost place. I whip my head around and see who's outside the car humming. There's no one there but that's impossible. I can *hear* it.

"Okay, you hear that right?" I say, stopping long enough to take the top off of my water bottle so I can see how much I have left. "You can hear that humming now, right? What song is that?

"I..I don't hear anything," Jason mumbles.

"You might as well get the hell out of here."

Why don't we go for a little walk

"Please don't talk." I say. Not now. I need to think. Jason is already gone and I'm standing here holding the driver's door open. I don't see where he went. He's just not here anymore and that's just fine with me. I can't see him anywhere and I wonder if maybe he was never there in the first place.

I start walking up the street towards the old school house. Behind me, the Mustang waits patiently and it depresses me so bad I could fling myself off of the University Bridge.

I take a long drink instead. Almost the same thing, I guess.

THIRTEEN

It's still pretty early so there are a lot of people out. They are mostly students either heading to or from the campus. I stand at the corner with a group of them, waiting to cross University Drive. There are three Asian girls, a guy around my age, and an older man with a mustache.

The Asian girls are busy talking in Chinese or Japanese, whatever it is. They don't stop long enough to even breathe. Just talking and talking so damn fast I wonder how any of them make sense of anything.

They are annoying the hell out of the older guy too, I can tell. He keeps looking over at them with this look on his face like he's going to pull a gun out and shoot them right in the street or something. He glances up at me and I nod. "Fucking chinks," he mutters.

I put my head down and pretend I never heard him. I mean, the girls were just standing there talking or whatever, there was no reason to go and get crazy. I wonder if he might have had some run-in with some Asians at some time or something, or got beat out of a job by one of them. With some people it doesn't take much, I guess. There are lunatics everywhere, you know.

I look up again, careful not to make eye-contact with Hitler. I look over at the other young guy. He has his earphones in, listening to music. If he heard the older guy's comment, it didn't seem to bother him. His world is perfect.

The light changes and we all cross the street. The Asian girls are laughing again, blissfully unaware. I think about following them to see if the mustache man will do anything. I doubt it. People like him *never* do anything. They just like to say comments like that under their breath and fantasize about what they *would* do if they had the chance. If he did do something, I will have no problem shooting him. He'd come up behind the girls and maybe push them or yank their hair, screaming the word chink over and over. There would be no sense trying to reason with his insanity. I'll take my gun out and rid the world of the magpie. I'll have to cry about it and be all sad when the police come but deep down everyone will be glad.

We don't need people like him around anyway.

With the way the world is nowadays, it seems like everyone is racist. Everybody is so scared of everyone else. It makes people crazy and then they do stupid things. Maybe we really should just segregate ourselves according to beliefs or race, or whatever it is that separates us. Build real walls around the different groups and not just imaginary ones. Of course, people would still send rockets over the walls at the other groups. That's just the way we are. And eventually, because people never stop putting up walls, our chosen group would get smaller and smaller until everyone was alone. In their own private kingdom. Hating everyone else outside their wall.

We're crazy sometimes. I swear we are.

I'm Métis or whatever but I'm not really sure what this means. I know it means a mixture of Native and European ancestry, and I know it's from my mom's side, but that's really all I can tell you. It's not like I grew up with the culture or anything. I didn't really even know anything about it until I was in Grade Four and we were studying the Riel Rebellion out at Batoche. The boys in the class got all into it because we got to re-enact this battle the Métis had with the North West Mounted Police. The class was split up into two sides and we got to shoot pretend guns at each other one afternoon. I was on the Métis side, which lost, and I remember being sort of pissed about it. I told my mom and she told me all about my relatives and my Métis bloodlines and that I should be proud to be Métis. We never really talked about it again though so I wasn't sure what I was supposed to be proud of.

I am near the old school house. I walk over to it, rubbing my hand along the stone wall. The windows and doors have been bordered up and I wonder if it was used for anything anymore. I decide that when I have a little money I'll buy this place and turn it into a school again.

I lean against the wall and have a nice little drink. The vodka fills my mouth and burns my throat. Kicking at the fallen leaves that cover the grass surrounding the old building, I wonder what the kids played at recess when they were here. I bet no one could tell me because people never remember anything like that.

Two girls walk by, their eyes trained on me as I kick away at all the dead leaves. "Get back to school," I yell. "You get back here or you'll pick the switch I beat you with." I was smiling while I was shouting so that they know I am joking. They don't say anything. They just hurry along the sidewalk, whispering back and forth to each other. One of them looks back at me and I raise my bottle in some sort of odd salute.

I see a few other students looking at me and I decide I better cool it for a while. I mean, I was just fooling around, but I remember the damn university cops. They would think I was acting 'drunk and disorderly' and the last thing I need was a phone call home or a night in the drunk tank.

I go back over to the sidewalk and start walking towards the larger buildings in the distance. I have never been on the University of Saskatchewan campus so I don't know my way around. It doesn't really matter. Maybe I'll check out the bar, maybe the library. I don't know.

On my left I pass this huge gothic castle looking building. A sign out front reads 'College of Medicine.' The three Asian girls from before are busy chatting away again on the stone steps leading up to the front door. I look around but I don't see my buddy Hitler anywhere. I bet he went and hung himself in one of the washrooms after he saw the Asian girls stop here. Maybe they will study his body in one of their medical classes later on.

Three younger guys walk by me and I sort of bump into them on account of the fact that I am staring up at the 'College of Medicine' castle. "Sorry," I said, because I always say sorry.

"You all right, man?" One of them said. He is dressed in tight jeans, converse shoes, a jean jacket over top of an obscure band t-shirt. The magpie chasing the tinsel and thinking he's different than everyone else.

"Yes," I say.

"You looking for something?"

At first I think he means drugs and I remember that I still have Jason's damn weed in my pocket. "No," I said.

"Alright, bro," he said, turning away to rejoin his friends.

"Hey," I walk towards him. "Where's the library? I have this big report due on Métis culture and I can't find the damn library."

"Just over there," he laughs, his eyes locked on my water bottle. "You see that tall building right across from us?" he said, pointing behind me. "It's right there."

"Thanks."

I watch as the kid runs back over to his friends. He says something to them and they all turn to look at me.

"You guys want to go for a few at the bar?" I shout, smiling again so they don't think I am a total freak. "On me."

"No bro," the first guy said. "We're good."

I start walking again, my eyes trained on the tall building that is supposed to be the library. It is about six stories tall and looks like the perfect place to chill out for a while. I could relax for a bit. Maybe have a few drinks while I read a couple of books or something. I could finally think about what I want to do next instead of having to rush all over the damn place.

I think that a university library will probably have a book or two on Métis culture and since I am here anyway, I should look one up. I don't know the first thing about how to do that though. I used to go to the public library back in the day with my mom and I imagine looking up books there was probably no different than here. We used to go to the library all the time actually. I was still pretty young so I'd wonder around the kid's section and flip through stupid little picture books because I didn't have the patience to sit and read just one book. I mean I *could* sit and read just one book but only if it was the only book available. If there was a bunch a books and I had to choose one, I couldn't do it. I was always worried that I might pick the wrong one and miss out on some great story I would have loved. Instead, I'd try to read them all, or at least a little bit from each one. It used to drive me crazy sometimes.

Mom and me stopped going to the library pretty abruptly and I'm not really sure why. My brother told me, years later, that mom only went there because she thought there were secret messages being sent to her through all the books she read. I guess that could have been true, given how my mom turned out, but my brother might have also made it up. He was always making up shit like that about her. Especially once she was gone and couldn't call him on his bullshit. Either way, mom never talked about it, so I'll never know the truth.

I wait at the cross walk again as a couple of cars drive by. I don't see any U of S cops yet so that's good. Maybe I'm stumbling and walking funny and I don't know it. They could drive by and pick me up before I even got into the damn school. Luckily, four or five students arrive at the cross walk and I am able to blend in with them as we cross the street.

The group of students is talking about some class they are all in. To be honest, I can barely understand a damn thing they are talking about. Physics or something. Whatever it was, they made me feel like I am a little kid. I mean, they don't look that much older than me but the way they are talking you would think they are all university professors.

I take a few sips from my drink as we walk.

The group of them stop at the bus stop and I continue on. I don't think I could have listened to them for a second longer. They were depressing the shit out of me. I feel like I am supposed to be talking like them by now, or at least understanding what they are saying, and I'm not ready. I never grew up.

I walk into the lobby of the school, thankful for the warm rush of air that covers me. It wasn't *that* cold out, and I have my old coat on, but I am shivering like a wet dog. Just shaking all over. I stand there, in front of the doors, and let the warm air wash over me until I stop shaking and I can think. It still sort of smells like wet boots. Just like the elementary school in a way. Maybe some things never change.

I see a man in a booth directly in front of the elevators and stairs leading up to the library and I freeze. He is wearing a light blue shirt, like something a cop would wear, and I get nervous as hell because I will have to walk right by him if I want to go to the library. I stand against the wall and watch him for a while. Maybe I'm a little paranoid about everything because I soon realize he is just the damn library security and not the rent-a-cops. He's reading a book and looking pretty bored with life. Groups of kids walk by him on their way to and from the library.

I see a washroom to my left and I decide I better go and get rid of the weed in my pocket. Sooner or later I probably *would* run into a university cop and I don't need weed in my pocket when it happened.

I walk over to the washroom and push the door open. The place smells like cleaner and piss. Lucky for me, the washroom is empty, so I hurry over to the single stall and lock myself in. Placing my cup on the floor, I pull the weed out. I open the little bag carefully so I don't go and spill any all over the place. It empties out cleanly into the toilet and I give the little bag a few good shakes, making sure all of it is gone. I flush the toilet three times. The whole place smells like pot now, the thick scent coming up from the toilet.

I walk out of the stall and stuff the little bag into the garbage can. I wash my hands damn near twenty times, just scrubbing and scrubbing until I am sure they don't smell like weed anymore.

I happen to catch a little glance of myself in the mirror as I scrub. I look so strange. My long hair is all tangled and greasy and it hangs down in front of my face, which is ash white. There are dark black circles under my eyes and it looks like I haven't slept in days. I put my head down and continue washing so I don't have to look anymore.

Look at me

"I can't." I whisper quietly into the sink. "I'm not sure who you are."

Yes, you do I'm Faran Bird, and I'm you, and I'm your brother, and I'm Faran Bird and the police are coming to get you

Suddenly, the washroom door swings open and some guy walks in. He must have been holding his piss in for damn near a year because he already has his pants unzipped before he even gets to the urinal. The guy looks a little older than me and I notice that he has a nice beard. I have a thing for beards, don't ask me why.

As a kid I used to sit with my dad and play with his damn beard all day long. I guess I was just fascinated that people grew hair all over their faces for no good reason, I think. I don't know. I've always been fascinated by people who do things for no good reason. I remember thinking that I should grow one too, just like my old man, because people would take me seriously then and not treat me like another stupid kid. My mom said it would be a few more years yet before I could grow one and I remember that depressing the shit out of me because I wanted one now. I was never any good at waiting for things. I'm sort of still waiting for that damn beard. I mean, I shave and all, but I don't really *need* to. I just shave off the little sparse hairs because that's what you're supposed to do when you get to be my age.

The beard guy looks over his shoulder at me as I said, "You got a nice beard there."

"What's that?" he said.

"I was just saying you have an awesome beard," I take another sip of vodka.

"Thanks, bud," he tells me after several seconds of silence. I think that maybe he thinks I am bugging him or something. He zips his pants up and walks over to the other sink.

"Stupid essays," I say, shaking my head like I am really stressed out or something. "A guy has to damn near kill himself to finish one sometimes. I might as well blow my brains out right here in the washroom."

"Yeah," he agrees, looking back over at me. "What class is that?"

"English."

He starts washing his hands and I notice that he doesn't use any soap. He just runs his hands under the water for a few seconds and sort of rubs them a little. He is going through the motions because I am standing there and that's what people do in washrooms when someone is standing there. If he had been alone he would have just pissed and left, I could tell. Probably dirty piss hands all over this damn university, I bet.

"You going to the bar later?" I ask casually. "I know *I'm*

going. Need to relax a little after this one. I'd like to go off campus but no wheels so I'll probably stick around here, what's this bar called again?"

"Louis."

"Yeah. I'll end up going there for only about the thousandth time."

He doesn't say anything. He reaches over beside me and grabs some paper towel so he can dry off his dirty piss hands. He tosses the paper into the garbage can and starts heading back towards the door.

"See you later if you decide to head over there," I said to him as he walks out. He might not have heard me though because he doesn't answer.

I should leave the washroom but for some reason I don't. I'm feeling sort of comfortable there, with my drink and everything, and I don't feel like leaving. No one, other than beard guy, knew I was there and I feel safe. I could actually think a bit for once.

I pretend it is my prison cell. There are no windows or clocks so I'll never be able to tell what time it is. It's supposed to drive me crazy, not knowing, and this is all part of my punishment. I'm going on ten years in there already. My captors will let me go if I just confess. They are watching me now, from behind the mirror. There are usually two of them, sometimes three. Day after day they watch me, just hoping I'll confess. The thing is that I like it there. I could stay in that dirty cell for a hundred years if I really wanted. They're my prisoners in a way.

"Having fun boys," I whisper into the mirror, making sure not to look at my bloodshot eyes. "You catch the guy who's *actually* guilty yet?"

I'm tapping on the mirror just as the door to the washroom swings open again. It startles me out of my little fantasy pretty good and I damn near drop my drink. It is a native guy, around my age, I guess. He heads straight for the pisser. He has long black hair that is pulled back and braided into a pony tail. I have to admit that it looks pretty good but I wasn't going to go and compliment him on it, like I did the beard guy. It is one thing to compliment a guy on his beard but you shouldn't say anything about his hair. Especially when you're piss drunk in a washroom.

"How's it going?" I said to him as he walks over to the sink.

"Hey," he said. He turns on the sink and I watch as he puts a little soap on his hands, lathering them so that they would actually be clean after. It wouldn't really matter though because on the way out he'll touch the door handle that Beardy Piss-Hands touched. Braids might as well have washed his hands with the urinal puck.

"Hey, do you know a guy named Faran Bird?" I say suddenly. I think that maybe he might know him because Saskatoon is a small city.

He stops washing and looks at me, "No. I don't think so."

When I look back down at the sink I hear him humming. It's that tune I can't place and it makes me wonder if he knows more than he's letting on. I close my eyes and really concentrate on what the hell he's humming.

"Listen, are you sure you don't know Faran Bird? I have a message for him and I can't seem to find the bastard anywhere."

He grabs a paper towel and starts to wipe his hands off, "That's too bad," he says. "Pretty sure I've never heard of him."

"Well, do you know where I could pick up some stuff?"

"Stuff? Like drugs?" He says.

"Yeah."

"No, I don't know too much about that." He turns and walks out of the bathroom, humming that tune so quietly I can barely make it out. He touches the door handle, just like I knew he would, and I want to haul him back by his braid so he can wash his damn hands all over again. I keep quiet though and have a drink instead.

He probably didn't know Faran. Braids was a nice young university student and Faran Bird was a dirty magpie who only found his treasures in the trash. They probably never crossed paths.

I decide I don't want to spend another second in that washroom with the dirty door handle and the pot toilet.

"Fine," I shout into the mirror at my imaginary captors, my finger thrust out in front of me like a gun. "I did it, and I'd do it again."

I grab the door handle with the sleeve of my coat and quietly leave the washroom.

FOURTEEN

I'm very interested in finding a book on the Métis. There has to be one in the library. How can a guy belong to a certain group and not know anything about it all. Not one thing. That's something a bloody magpie would do.

I stand in front of the elevator and try to decide what floor of the library I want to go to. I know it doesn't really matter, and that I could have found a damn book to read on any floor, but for some reason I can't decide. I just stand there looking at the numbers.

"One, two, three, four, five, six, seven" I whisper.

A girl comes up beside me. Out of the corner of my eye, I watch her watching me. I know she is waiting for me to pick a damn number and it is bugging the shit out of me. I am getting all nervous and my head is itching like crazy again. I say, "Go ahead," motioning towards the floor numbers.

She whispers something I can't make out before stepping forward and pushing the button for floor two. She shakes her head like she has made a mistake and pushes floor three.

What's she doing

I notice what she does. "Why did you do that?"

She looks at me carefully. "He made a mistake. I meant to push floor three." She smiles sheepishly at me.

He made a mistake

"Who made a mistake?" I say. I'm very uncomfortable but I try to act casual. I don't want her to know I know what the hell she's doing.

She looks confused. "No, I just hit the wrong button and…"

"You hit number twenty-three. Very clearly you did that as soon as you knew I was watching." I wonder if she recognizes me from somewhere and is trying to bug me about my brother. Maybe she's from my high school and I don't recognize her. She might have been one of the magpies trying to fit in by bugging me and my brother and when he was twenty-three. The last year I ever got to hear his voice.

"I don't know what you mean." She looks scared and I realize I'm crowding her.

Go to the last year of twenty-three because you can't just stand here when you don't have a reason

I hear a small ding and seconds later the elevator doors open. She is watching me again and she won't follow me into the elevator. I know it's because I have to go alone. This is a special place reserved only for me. I see a slight smile form on her face just as the elevator door slides slowly closed.

Now I am in the library. I am in the last year of twenty-three.

The floor is in the shape of a giant rectangle with little desk cubicles lining the walls. The middle of the floor is lined with bookshelves. Masquerading as books, the memories of a short and tragic life sit silently waiting. They smell of dust and paper and look much older than twenty-three years. I feel their worn and weathered spines against my fingertips as I stroll down the aisle. Their titles are a mystery and a riddle and if you never knew him, you would never understand what they mean.

My hand comes to rest on a book. The title reads *As I Lay Dying* by William Faulkner. I laugh and the sound bends and stretches around these strange walls. "Really? Is that some sort of joke?" I say.

You got me little buddy

"Don't you have better things to do than bug me?"

Do I ever

I laugh again and continue my walk. There is a contentment I feel as I move in just being here and for a brief moment in time I forget about Faran Bird and Saskatoon and Oxycontin.

What are you doing here? Why don't we take a little walk

I ignore any whispers of doubt and decide that there is still important work to do. I need to find answers in and amongst the pages of this place.

"Show me how to access this place." I say as calmly as I can stand it. Yet, even before I'm done speaking I feel like I already know the answer. The pages and the numbers are more important than the covers because the covers are what people want us to see. A magpie will spend his whole life working on his cover just so you'll never look at what's inside the pages. His true story.

Hey

I slip into a small cubicle against the wall. The little stall has a window so I can look outside but the frosted glass is hard to look out of and all I see is blackness. I grab a random book from off the adjacent shelf because it doesn't matter what book I read from in this place.

The book cover reads *Sociology of the Modern Family*.

I think about opening it on page one but I change my mind. It won't be clear if I read it like that. All it would do was get me depressed. First, because I probably wouldn't understand what it was saying, and second, because anything I did understand would make me think about my own family. The sociology of my modern family.

I turn to page twenty-three.

It is in the middle of a chapter but it doesn't matter what came before or what comes after. All that matters is here.

I place my finger along the page and quietly read aloud, *"with damage inflicted by multiple family transitions."* Words along the page jump out at me, screaming for attention. *"Not the fault of the caregiver."*

Who then? I wonder. "Whose fault is any of it?

"Questions will arise as to who will become the primary caregiver."

I close the book in anger. "There are no questions. You left me alone to be my own damn primary caregiver."

We are all our own damn primary caregiver

"I was too young to handle any of that. I try to remember how old I even was. Twelve, I guess. I was just twelve-years-old which doesn't seem right because at the time I felt so young. There were times though when I felt much older. When the house smelled like vomit and stale beer and cigarettes and I would throw an old blanket on my passed out father. I felt so much older then.

I turn to page twelve.

"different periods of time when a disruptive or broken home has been used to explain why children can become delinquent but this is not always this case."

"I'm not delinquent," I laugh at the absurdity of it all. "You of all people must *know* that."

The pages of the book feel so strange in my hand. I'm not completely sure they're even real. It would be so much easier just to put the book down and go home.

"it is not the fault of the child."

I stare hard at the words. "Is that your idea of an apology? Do you think that I believe any of this is my fault? It's not my fault at all."

It's not your fault at all

I close the book and place it on the desk in front of me. I want to read more because there are so many books here. There are so many answers but I'm not even sure of the questions anymore.

Kill Faran Bird

"How will that change anything?" I feel like I'm yelling at all these whispering voices but my voice is getting lost somewhere in the void. My skin is suddenly very itchy and this place is no longer comfortable.

I hear the sound of approaching footsteps.

"Hey, are you all right?"

My eyes snap open and I turn to the side. "A girl, around my age, is standing in front of me. She holds her textbook in front of her chest like a shield. The textbook's title reads, *Psychology* and I wonder if she has been sent to this place or whether she has always been here.

"Do you need anything?" she asks carefully.

"I have all that I need." I look at her blonde hair and pale blue eyes, trying to place her. There is something familiar in her face but I can't remember. She must be here for a reason though because you can't just come into a place like this if you don't have a reason.

The girl with the pale blue eyes waits for a few moments before she quietly disappears. I'm not completely sure she was even real. There was something *too* familiar in her eyes and I think I must have made her up.

Slowly, I stand, and make my way down another aisle. I leave *Sociology of the Family* behind because there are just so many other books. I wonder what books will fill my library one day.

I take twelve steps and then twelve more because they equal twenty-four. The year that was to come. I grab the book directly to my right and turn to page twenty-three without even looking at the cover.

"he would often smoke cigarettes as he pondered these very questions."

"Just tell me what to do." I say between gritted teeth. "None of this is clear to me."

I told you what to do

Ahead of me two people came into view. Young guys, around my age. They are looking for something together on the shelf. They are whispering back and forth to each other and I am too far away to make out what they are saying. I move towards them, counting my steps as I do. When I have taken the required twelve, I stop and listen as they talk in that horrible hurried whisper.

"He knows what to do." One of the guys said.

"How do you know?" his partner replies.

"Because we already told him."

I keep my eyes on the wall of books because I'm too afraid to look at them. "What did you say?" I'm not sure if I thought my words or yelled them but whatever it was, they hear them.

They are silent for several seconds and then the first guy speaks. "Nothing. We're just looking for a book."

I decide I need to leave. It's becoming jangled and blurred around the edges and if I'm not careful I'm going to go crazy. Honestly, I will. Forgetting my steps, I brush past the two guys, making sure not to make eye-contact with either of them in case there is a familiarity in them. Rows and rows of bookshelves are everywhere and I swear they're multiplying so as to block my path to the elevator. I'm not supposed to leave yet but I can't stand another minute. I keep my head down move forward. I concentrate on the sound of my shoes as they scuff along the smooth linoleum that doesn't have a memory.

"Just let me go," I whisper.

You know what to do

"I am going to do it. I told you that."

The suddenly, the elevator is in front of me. I am allowed to leave.

I push the button and wait. I need a drink and this is the only real clear thought in my mind.

FIFTEEN

Down here in the lobby of the library I feel much better. I am grounded and things seem to make a little more sense. I need a drink and I figure this will be my first priority. A calm mind is a focused mind, after all.

I don't know where the bar is so I continue to walk aimlessly through the school. There is a staircase ahead of me so I follow it down. My legs feel weak and rubbery beneath me and for a moment I think I might pass out. I try to remember the last time I have eaten anything. Yesterday? The day before? I can't remember.

Three guys are talking near the bottom of the stairs. Two of the guys are wearing bright red jackets with an 'Engineering' patch on the arm. The other guy is a cowboy or something. He's not wearing a hat or anything but he has that big buckle they always wear and the tight jeans.

I step off the staircase and walk over to them. They are busy talking about some bullshit but they are being really quiet about it so I don't hear what they are saying. "Hey, how much for a ticket?" I smile.

"What?" the Engineering student said.

"How much to ride the train there, Mr. Engineer?" I am grinning like a clown so that he knows I am joking. He doesn't smile back so I guess he doesn't get it. "You know, because you drive fucking trains for a living because you're an engineer."

The engineer looks over at John Wayne before turning back to me. He is staring at me like I am a nutcase and I laugh out loud at the thought. "How's it going?" H e says carefully.

"I'm good. I was just kidding around about the whole engineering thing. Sort of a double meaning with the word. The stupid English language is full of them, isn't it?" I try to think of another example but I can't come up with anything that quick. "It's like they couldn't figure out what to call something so they just started re-using words."

"Help you out with something?" John Wayne said. His voice is kind of high-pitched and doesn't match the way he looks at all. That's why he probably dresses like a cowboy in the first place, so that people don't think he's a queer or something.

"You guys know where the bar is?"

"Louis?" Mr. Engineer asks.

"Yeah, Louis Riel's."

"You just go through here," he said, pointing to another small staircase. "Then go up the escalators and out the main doors to your right. Go outside and keep walking left and you'll run right into it."

"Thanks. Listen, you guys want to come with me? On me, seriously. I'm stressed over this report I have to do and I don't know a damn thing about the subject. Not one damn thing."

Mr. Engineer looked over at his cowboy buddy again.

"Not tonight, man. We're heading over to the arcade for a while." John Wayne said.

I don't feel like explaining why I hate video games and how I can't understand the point of them at all. It won't matter what I say anyway because they'd still play them. It's like parents warning their children not to do drugs or drink or something. In one ear and out the other. Drugs and drink just like mom and dad do.

I turn and start following their directions. As I walk, I notice how deserted this place is and it makes me sort of happy. I am a ghost again and I am haunting these halls. I am looking for my damn book and I'll never be able to rest in peace if I can't find it. These are not my old playgrounds though. I am a stranger in a foreign land.

The escalators are turned off because it must be late. I have to walk up them and I notice again how weak and tired I feel. When this is all over, and I can finally go home again, I think I'll end up sleeping for days. Every few hours I'll wake up just long enough to pour a few ounces down my throat and read a couple of words from my Métis book, if I ever find one. My demons will be gone and I can finally sleep.

I realized I must have been directly underneath the library because I can see the bus stop through the glass exit doors to my right. There are a few people waiting inside for the bus and a couple more are outside. The outsiders are smoking, tiny little cancer sticks clutched tightly between their fingers. I wonder how many of them want to quit but can't because you had to do *something* when you are standing outside.

I remember the cigarette that Jason had given me. Unzipping my coat pocket, I reach inside and pull the smoke out. I push the door open and walked outside.

My cigarette feels weird and foreign in my hand and I wish I had practiced with it a little. Smokers always look so casual when they're holding their smokes. I know enough not to hold it with just my thumb and pointer finger, like a joint. That's a dead give-away of an amateur. I hold it between my middle and pointer fingers, trying hard not to squeeze it too much. As long as nobody thinks I'm some phony magpie pretending to smoke, I'll be fine.

I walk up to a couple of guys standing by the bus stop. They look a little older than me, but not by too much. "You got a light?" I say, casual as shit.

"Yeah," said the guy. He is really tall and thin and he has the hood of his dark black jacket, whatever the fuck you call it, pulled up over his head. He reaches into the pocket of his jeans and pulls out a small metallic lighter.

"Thanks," I said, leaning over and letting him light the smoke for me. I hold the cigarette in my mouth and try to look like I have been smoking for years. Probably die of cancer any day now. I have to be careful not to breathe in so I don't go and cough all over the damn place. I feel like I am five-years-old or something, standing out there, pretending to smoke.

"I'm Daniel," said the tall guy in the black jacket. He recently had a haircut because his edges are razor sharp. I wonder if he actually had *needed* a haircut or whether he always looked like he just had a haircut. This fact will tell others a lot about you.

We make our introductions and even though I hear the other guy's name, I can't recall it seconds later. Charlie or Barclay, I don't know. I might have remembered if I hadn't been staring at these tattoos that Daniel has on his hands. They are done up to look like he had skeleton hands. In dark black ink, starting at the tips of his fingers and running up the length of his hands so that it looks like all his flesh has rotted away. The tattoo might continue all the way up his whole body for all I know but I can't tell because of his jacket. He sees me looking at the ink work and I worry he might think I am impressed with it.

"Is that the bar over there?" I said, pointing behind us at another gothic castle looking building in the distance. I can hear muffled music coming from somewhere within.

"Yeah," Daniel answered, taking a long drag on his cigarette. "Are you heading over there? Dollar draft night."

I can smell beer on his breath.

"I think so. You guys?"

"Already been there," Charlie or Barclay said. "It's not that busy tonight anyway, because of finals."

"Yeah, I think I could go for a few," I said. "Stressed out from studying and all."

We stand there and shoot the shit for a couple of minutes. I'm not really listening to them all that much. I am busy trying to smoke properly and it's nice because I don't have to talk. I can just stand here and smoke. I tap off my butts like a pro. I could probably pass for a senior student.

I notice that Daniel has more tattoos on his neck. I can't tell what they look like because the area isn't well lit. I bet they are stupid and if I see them I won't be able to think of anything else.

I hate tattoos. I can't think of anything I hate more about my generation than tattoos. It's not the actual idea of them. Not at all. They *could* be a good idea and but young people are too stupid and they always take a good thing and screw it up. In the summer I watch all of the magpies as they flaunt themselves around town. They copy slogans and wrap their arms in tribal art and write stupid quotes in six inch letters on their chest. It used to have more meaning back when only a few people had them. Bikers and heavy metal dick heads, people like that. Now, everyone has them, and they don't mean anything. They don't *mean* anything at all. Sure, they'll tell you every tattoo they have means something but all it really means is that they don't know anything. You don't flip through a tattoo book for a half hour and find one that really means anything. You just want it to mean something because what kind of person would you be if you just marked up your body for no good reason. What would everyone else think? That's all they really care about. Everyone needs a reason. It's better to have your skin clear and empty. Pure. I think that there's more meaning in that than any tattoo I've ever seen.

Like saying fuck-you all day long

I hear a cold whisper just along the edge of my mind and I know I need to keep it quiet for a bit longer. I need music, a drink. Something other than just these two.

I glance over at Daniel as he said, "I would have stayed longer but no one wants to drink alone."

"I would have stayed," Daniel's buddy smiles sheepishly. "I'm too busy with school."

Every young person I ever met thinks they're too damn busy for everything.

"I'll drink with you," I said. "I mean, I'm going anyway so you might as well come." I might be a little pushy maybe. I don't know. It's just that I am getting a little edgy and nervous sitting out here and I need a drink in me. "I'll buy."

Daniel looks over at his friend and they both laugh. I don't know if they are laughing at me or the situation or both. I don't really care.

"C'mon, just for a while," I said. "No one likes to drink alone."

"Fuck it," Daniel said, throwing his cigarette butt to the ground and stamping it out. "I'll go for a bit."

I drop my smoke to the concrete and start walking towards the bar. I guess I want to hurry things along because I don't want him to go and change his mind or anything. I also want a drink really bad, even if it is just cheap draft beer.

I watch as Daniel said goodbye to his friend. He then turns and runs towards me, the glare from the streetlight on his back so that I can't see his face. His black hood slips off and billows behind him as he runs and for a moment I think he looks familiar. Like I have gone for a drink with him a thousand times before.

SIXTEEN

Before we walked in, I thought the whole castle was the bar. It turns out that the bar is just downstairs. I follow Daniel down the stairs. I suddenly remember Jason telling me all about campus bars and I.D.

I tried to find someone who could hook me up with fake I.D. a few times but it never really worked out. The look and feel of the paper was always wrong and I was sure I could have got the same results with a damn photocopier. If I ever *do* find a legit source, I'll probably start a new life. Move out west somewhere. Print up a driver's license and a couple of degrees maybe. Find myself a new name. I wonder how many other people would do the same thing if they had the chance. Leave their self behind. Not tired of life. Tired of something.

We come to a small doorway and I follow behind Daniel as close as I can stand it. Just as simple as that, we are in the bar. There was no door man or security or anything. I want to phone Jason and tell him he's stupid.

The bar is half-full maybe. Half-empty. Strange brew of black-haired emo punks, preppy assholes in Lacoste polos, nowhere kids, and hipsters in band t-shirts. It feels like every other bar I've ever been to in Saskatoon. A dirty old magpie convention.

The bar is decorated in metal and chrome, like we have come to get drunk in a damn spaceship or something. It smells of sweat and alcohol and fried food. An old R.E.M. song is playing over the speakers and the sound is just loud enough for me to hide in for a while.

Daniel sits down at a glass and metal table meant for four. I nod at him and head towards the bar. A slutty looking blonde is behind the counter. She is laughing at some joke she shares with some other slutty looking blonde that works there. I squeeze in between two guys who smell of hair gel and too much cologne.

"What can I get you?" The blonde said. I notice her heavy make-up that she wears to hide the little bit of acne that she has. From a distance you might have thought she was pretty but up close, with the make-up, and the acne, she is just another trashy blonde. I think if she hadn't been wearing make-up, and not trying to hide her damn zits and all, someone would think she was not too bad. Maybe even beautiful.

She is looking into the kitchen as I say, "I need two pitchers of whatever is on sale?"

She doesn't reply. Instead, she reaches underneath the counter and pulls out two empty pitchers. She walks over to the beer taps and I see one of her legs dip to the side so that she almost falls right on her face. She's wearing these dumb heels, damn near six inches tall, and she can't walk properly in them. You can tell that she probably grew up in a small town or something, maybe even a farm, and that she has never worn high heels in her whole stupid life. She acts like it is no big deal but I bet she wants to hang herself. She's lucky though because no one saw it but me and I don't care about things like that.

She places the two pitchers on the counter in front of

me and takes the money I have left for her. She returns moments later with my change.

"Can I get three shots of something? " I said.

"Shots of what?"

"I don't know."

That's one of the reasons why I hate drinking in bars. All of the shots you order have some stupid name and you feel like a real asshole when you order them. When I own a bar I'm going to have a shot called 'The Saskatoon'. It's going to be made up of a little bit of everything all mixed together. After you drink it, you will sit around and think you're cultured and better than everyone else and that maybe you should buy a 'loft' like all the people out east. The alcohol will wear off quickly though, and then you'll remember that you're just a dumb ass hick from the prairies and that Saskatoon is not New York or Toronto or Vancouver, no matter how much you want it to be. You will have to keep on ordering 'The Saskatoon' all night just so you don't feel like such a piece of shit. I'll be a millionaire.

"Like a China White or..."

"Just three shots of whiskey. Plain whiskey.

She looks at me funny before she reaches back under the counter and pulls out three shot glasses. She pours quickly and perfectly, not a drop wasted, and I think again that she must have grown up in a small town.

I pick up the first shot and drink it. I don't drink a lot of whisky so I sort of forget what it tastes like. I cough as the warmth of the drink spreads throughout my body. I probably would have bought more whisky if it didn't smell so much. It's much harder to hide than gin or vodka. You can smell someone twisted on whiskey half-way down the street and it lingers a while after you drink it.

I think it must come out of your pores or something, I don't know. Gin and vodka smell too. Don't believe that bullshit that they don't. It's just a different kind of smell, not as potent.

"Aren't you a little warm in that coat?" She asks.

I pick up the second shot and drink it before I say, "Not really. I sort of have to wear it on account of all the scars."

You have important work to do

She is listening to me. "What happened?"

"The war. Afghanistan." Everybody here would soon have diplomas and degrees but none of them will have scars like I do. That's all that *really* matters in the end.

"My brother is thinking of joining the army," she said. She is trying to wipe off the counter with this dirty old dish rag or something and it is really bugging me. The rag looks like someone has just given the toilets a quick wipe down with it and I can't stop thinking about all of the shit she is wiping all over the place. I take my hands off of the metal surface of the counter.

I look behind me and see Daniel watching me. He's probably wondering what the hell I am doing but I don't care. I'm giving the bastard free beer. He can wait all night for all I care. I smile and wave at him as I drink the last shot.

"Table twelve," the blond yells to one of her partners.

I look up from my drink and try to catch her eye but her focus is not on me.

"Twelve," she says again, motioning with her hand.

"What are you talking about?" I say, watching her face carefully.

"What?" she says to me.

"You were going on about table twelve."

"Oh, yeah," she says, resuming her mindless wiping

with the dirty rag. "There's a bunch of work to do on twelve."

I don't know what she means and I sit there for a moment trying to figure it all out. "You tell your brother to be careful out there." I finally tell her.

"What?" She is looking behind me at something and I can't make eye-contact with her so she could see how serious I am being.

"Your brother. Tell him to be careful."

"Careful about what?"

"The war."

She continues to wipe. "Yeah, okay."

I grab the handles of the two pitchers of beer and walk back over to Daniel. The whisky is really flying through my bloodstream now and my legs don't feel as weak or as tired as before. Things are sharper and more in focus and my own thoughts are the only ones I hear.

I carefully place the pitchers down on the table as I say, "Sorry about that, she was giving me a hard time."

"What'd she want?" He takes one of the pitchers of beer and pours it into a pint glass.

"She was hitting on me," I said. I fill my glass with the other pitcher and take a nice long swallow. "She made me have a few shots with her."

He lifts his pint with his skeleton hands and takes a drink. He doesn't thank me or anything for the beer, like it was a real damn honor just to be having a cold one with him or something. I know it doesn't really mean much, but you should always thank a guy for buying you a drink. No one has any manners anymore.

"Which one?" He looks up at the bar.

"I don't know. The blonde one."

"You get her number?"

"She tried to give it to me but I told her to keep it," I said. I stopped long enough to drain half of my glass. "I've already got a lady. Besides, I don't date bar girls." I said it like I had a lot of experience with girls. The truth is that I don't really have any experience at all. I mean, I guess I have a few friends that are girls, but nothing you'd classify as a romantic relationship. Girls don't see me that way. I don't see me that way. I can barely stand being around myself too long. I couldn't imagine being married to someone and having them bug the shit out of me for forty years. It would never happen. It's safe to say I'll be a life-long bachelor. No one wants to marry a twelve-year-old.

Daniel is looking around the bar and I can tell he is pretty bored with me. It's not like it was a real treat for me either but at least I am trying. Something I always do when I need someone to hang out with, and they're not really into it, is I get them to talk about themselves. Magpies will go on for hours if you let them. The key is to not talk about your own shit too much. People are assholes and they don't care about you or what you think. They're just waiting for their turn to talk. So I always make it their turn.

"You a student here or something?" I ask.

"No." Daniel sips at his beer and keeps looking around the bar like it is the most interesting thing in the world. It's like talking to a bloody post.

"What do you do then?"

"I'm a musician. Singer and lead guitar player."

I know he plays metal. I can just tell. He has a metal vibe to him. I'm not a huge metal fan but I know enough to pretend for a while.

"Right on. You in a band?"

"Yeah. We're called 'Battle Axe.'"

"Metal?" I ask, as if they play country with a stupid name like that.

"Fucking rights," he said. "You into metal?"

"Fucking rights," I said. "Better than rap."

"Don't get me started," he said, flipping his hair out of his face not because he needs to but because he thinks it looks cool. He has an audience now and there really is no point if one doesn't have an audience. "Rap isn't even music. It's just a few steps up from those tribal assholes beating their drums out in the middle of Africa. That's why the Indians like it too. Built into their genetic make-up to like music like that."

I sit in silence, unsure of what to say.

"Yeah, you know what I'm talking about. I hate Indians."

I really get uncomfortable around racists. I feel like I want to debate them or something but I don't know what to say.

"I don't know about that," I said. "We dropped on in here and sort of screwed around with them pretty good, like with their culture and stuff."

"Their culture? Chasing buffaloes around and sleeping in teepees while they moved from place to place isn't culture. The bastards would still be doing it too if we hadn't shown up."

He said it like he was the first one off the boat from Europe or something.

"Yeah, maybe." I feel like I am a part of the Native population right now. I mean, technically I always have been, but right now I feel like I am back in Grade Four and we're re-enacting the Battle of Batoche. This time I am happy with the side I am on. Except it still feels like I'm not on any side. Never mind being picked last,

I wasn't picked at all. I am White. I am Native. I am nothing.

I think about Daniel's words. Of course the Natives would still be living like that. If it worked for them why would they go and change it. What's with everybody's obsession with changing things all of the time. If something works for a guy then he should leave it alone. You start messing around with your original plan too much in some sort of attempt to make it better and pretty soon you don't even know what you're trying to make better any more. You forget your plan as you plow forward in the name of progress. I bet you that there wasn't any depression in the Native population back then. Before everyone came and changed everything. A guy knew what he wanted out of life and what he had to do. Then, when the white guys showed up they said, 'No, that's not good enough. You're not progressing. Do it like us.' Now everyone's depressed because they don't know what they're supposed to be doing to be happy. Wake up. Go to work all day and make money. Buy things. Buy better things because if you don't, you're not progressing and adapting to the change, which means you are not happy. Chasing the carrot of happiness until we die depressed and wondering what the point of it all was. Before everything went and changed, Natives were probably happy all the time, I'll bet.

I empty my pint glass and immediately reach for the pitcher. "You guys play around Saskatoon?" I need to change the subject before I go insane.

Daniel is looking around the bar again, "What?" He said. The rap or hip-hop song pounds out of the speakers and the dance floor starts to fill with people.

"Your band. I was asking if you guys play around

Saskatoon much." The music is really loud and it's making me nervous as hell for some reason.

"Sort of."

This guy is something else. A real conversationalist. I'm regretting asking him to have a few drinks with me.

"You see that over there," he said, pointing behind me at two preppy looking guys on the dance floor. The two guys are dancing pretty close, I guess, and every once in a while they sort of touch each other. They are gay and you could *tell* they're gay from a mile away but it's no big deal. Who gives a shit. I mean, people in my generation don't really care too much about that anymore. Some people are gay. Get over it. There are gay people everywhere you go. If you start worrying about something as stupid as that, you'll go crazy enough to jump off a building.

"Yeah, what about them?"

"Fucking queers. They make me sick."

"Yeah," I said. I sip my beer and wonder why he has come here in the first place. I could ask him but he'll never give me the *real* answer anyway.

"At Bud's those two fags would be dragged outside and taught a lesson."

I've been to Bud's a few times. Dingy looking place on Broadway that specializes in music acts. A lot of metal bands play there and on most weekends the place is filled with morons. I was there last year and got into a bit of trouble. I was wearing this red shirt, which is a big no-no at a place like that. You have to wear a black t-shirt and have a shit load of tattoos. Official dress code. I was in line, trying to get a drink, and this idiot poured a drink on me. He called me a faggot and told me to get out of the bar. I was alone and I left because I didn't feel like getting my ass kicked. I could have been there with my own personal army and I would have left. I didn't even want to be there anyway. I just happened to be on Broadway and I had wanted a drink. I just wanted to hide in the sounds for a while and be left alone.

"Doesn't that shit bug you?" Daniel takes a drink. He's pounding it back as good as me. He is gripping the hell out of his pint glass and the veins in his stupid skeleton hands are bulging. He is a lunatic. Probably gay himself, which is why he's so damn worked up about everything.

"I don't know," I said casually. "As long as they're not trying to do anything gay to me, I don't really give a shit." Daniel looks at me and I see a little flash of anger in his eyes. I think he was about to say something but he stops himself and takes a drink instead.

I gulp some more beer and continue. "Everybody is gay. Everyone and everything, don't you know?" I'm just joking around with him because I know it will piss him off. I really don't know why I do that so much. It's like I'm addicted to pissing people off.

"I'm not queer." I watch him shifting in his seat and I can tell he is pretty uncomfortable with the whole thing.

"I'm not saying you're a homosexual. I'm saying you're gay. Everyone is gay."

"What the fuck does that mean?" He reaches for the pitcher again and pours another pint of beer. He splashes a little drink on the table and I can't tell if he did it because he's angry or drunk, or both.

"Everybody is in love with themselves. Everything is a competition and everyone thinks they're the best. I bet that's how the world will end. Eventually, no one will be able to fall in love with anyone but themselves. Relationships will be too demanding on a guy because no matter how much that person loves you, they won't love *everything* about you and you won't understand it. Only you can love everything about you. Unless they can clone themselves, people will stop having kids because they won't be perfect replicas of themselves. Everyone will die and the world will end because everyone is gay. Do you ever think about stuff like that?"

Daniel is looking at me like *I* was the one that was the lunatic. "Do I ever think about what?"

"About how the world will end."

"Not really. Nuclear war probably."

"Hey, do you have any guitar strings on you?" I ask suddenly. I remembered him saying he was a guitar player.

"No. Why would I have guitar strings on me?"

"I don't know. I've been looking for guitar strings for a hundred years now. I can't play my guitar without any strings." I swallow some more beer and remember why I don't drink it all the time. My stomach feels swollen and bloated and I don't even feel all that drunk.

"I don't carry them around with me." He reaches into the chest pocket of his shirt and tosses something across the table at me. "Here, I have a guitar pick you can have. Best I can do."

I take the pick and look at it. Across the face there is a double-bladed axe, a small skull above it. The words 'Battle Axe' is scrawled along the top.

I start to feel kind of bad for the strange homophobic across from me who covers up himself with scary tattoos and plays in a heavy metal band because he was probably abused as a child or something. I imagine him getting together with his idiot band mates and designing this stupid little pick and being so damn proud of it that they pass them out to strangers in bars. I want to shoot him before he realizes the futility of it all and shoots himself. "The poor young musician was murdered," they'll say because it sounds better than, "The metal guy blew his own brains out because he was a racist, homophobic, asshole."

"Hey, you must know how to get drugs, I bet." I say it casually so he stays calm about the whole thing.

Daniel tilts his glass up and empties his pint once again. He is really hammering it down for some reason. Maybe he is depressed. Maybe he is trying to impress me. I don't know. People do all sorts of strange things when you let them.

"Yeah, I know a few people," Daniel said. "What are you looking for?"

"Well, I'm actually looking for a guy I get stuff off of all the time. I lost his number."

"What's his name?"

Faran Bird

I take a small sip from my drink and say, "Faran Bird."

Daniel laughs out loud and it carries over the heavy bass of the song playing in the background. "You don't know Faran Bird," he says with a smirk that makes me want to reach across the table and break his face.

"So you know who he is?" I have a hard time hiding my excitement because I thought it would take days before I could track him down.

"Yeah, I know who he is, but you obviously don't."

"What do you mean?"

"Bird Man doesn't sell drugs directly," Daniel smiles. "He's too high up for that. That's why I know you don't know him."

"He knows me," I say as calm as I can stand it.

Daniel shakes his head and grabs his pint of beer. He's

smiling between drinks and it makes me think of him as a child for some reason. I wonder what Daniel wanted to be when he grew up.

"So can you help me get in touch with him?"

Daniel looks at me and his smile slowly fades. "I can't do that," he said. "I don't get involved with the Indian gangs too much."

"I don't think you understand the importance of it all." I stare into his eyes so he can understand the meaning in my words but I don't think my message will ever make sense in his world. He notices my gaze and I think it bothers him because he nervously runs his hand through his slick black hair. His wet and oily hair. As dirty as any magpie there ever was.

"I can't do it." He says again a little more aggressively. He rises suddenly and announces that he has to piss. I watch him as he walks to the washroom. He is looking around at everyone as he moves through the bar. It's like he is waiting for someone to look at him wrong or something so he can act. That's another reason I don't like going out to drink. Too many guys like Daniel around. Unpredictable and chaotic.

He doesn't understands the importance of it all

I sigh, wishing my drinks had kept them at a bay a little longer. "I *know* he doesn't."

Make him understand the importance of it all

I grab my glass again and turn my attention back to the dance floor. More hip-hop is playing and the crowd seems really into it. I watch the two gay guys for a while and I sort of envy them. I mean, there they are, in the middle of the dance floor, and they don't give a fuck who is watching. Not one fuck. It's not like anyone cares anyway, except for Daniel, but the gay guys don't know that. They could have been in a bar full of guys like Daniel and I bet they would dance the exact same way. I can tell. I like to think that if I was gay I'd be able to do something like that, but I'm not sure I could. I know people too well and I'd be thinking about people like Daniel the whole time I was trying to dance. I would never be able to relax enough to just dance. It's all because I pay attention too much. I pay attention to everything and it's enough to drive me loony sometimes. I catch what everyone else misses. I wish I could be like them and just let everything miss me, but I can't. I know what everyone else doesn't know. I'd give anything to forget all the things that I know. To start over and be as innocent as the rest of these people. I could dance then. I could dance all night. Ignoring the magpies as they cawed at me from the sidelines.

Daniel comes back to the table. He drinks the rest of his beer quickly. Then, glaring at the dance floor one more time, he picks up his jacket and says, "I'm out of here."

I finish the rest of my beer and run to catch up to Daniel. I follow him back up the stairs and out the front doors of the building. As soon as we get outside he reaches into his coat pocket and pulls out a pack of cigarettes. As he lights up he says, "Guess we'll see you around then."

"Well hold on," I say. I'm smiling so he thinks everything is all right.

"What?"

I take a quick look around to make sure we're alone. Deciding that we are, I calmly reach into the waistband of my jeans and pull out my gun. I hold it out in front of me so that if I was to pull the trigger the bullet would catch poor Daniel somewhere in the chest. I've never actually pointed a gun at someone before and I'm surprised at how little I feel as I'm doing it. It's probably because I'm not going to shoot him so it feels as harmless as pointing my finger at him.

The importance of it all

"What the fuck are you *doing*? Daniel says, his arms instinctively rising up in a defensive position.

"Nothing at all. Turn around and go around the edge of the building." I'm surprised again at how calm I am. My voice sounds clear and sharp to my ears and I wonder what that means.

Daniel stands near a group of trees that line the wall of the bar. He is off the sidewalk and it is as dark as hell back here. The muffled beat of another rap song carries through the wall and I time my breathing with it so I can stay in focus with this reality.

"Don't shoot me," Daniel pleads.

"I'm not going to shoot you," I say. "The two faggots dancing in the bar are going to shoot you. I'm with them and we've been waiting for a magpie like you for a long time."

"What?" Daniel swallows and coughs lightly. "Fuck, man...I don't. I just said that stuff. I didn't mean it."

"Are you afraid of faggots, Daniel? Is that why you say things like that?" I hold the gun out in front of me as I walk towards him. I imagine I must look scary because the lights from the street are behind me. A black shadow of death inching towards him.

"I'm sorry," Daniel calls out with a shaky voice and I know he's scared. I feel bad because I don't want to scare him and I don't want to hurt him. Honestly, I don't. I just want him to understand the importance of it all.

"Keep still. Don't move your head an inch,"

'What do you want from me?" There's a pleading in his voice and it make me sick to hear it.

"I want you to keep still," I say again. I move slowly closer until my face is inches from his and my hand is pointing the gun towards the side of his head. I smell beer and cigarettes on his breath and in the moment I think of my brother. He comes to my room late at night to tell me a story. He smells of cheap beer and cigarettes and all his stories are bullshit but I love them anyway. I always loved them anyway.

"Please, what do you want?"

We found him in the garage in the car

I lean forward and press my mouth to Daniel's lips. I feel him recoil but he remembers my gun and stays still as I lightly rest it against his ear. My tongue slips into his mouth and in it I try to convey what it is I mean by it all. I kiss his eyes. His forehead. His lips one more time. I whisper into his ear, "I want you to tell me where to find Faran Bird."

Daniel is crying and I think of him on the playground as a child. "I don't...I don't fucking know, man." He mumbles.

"I think you do."

"I only met him a few times. He was staying off of Twentieth, I think." Daniel pauses, his mind racing to find an answer before I pulled the trigger. "No...it was Eighteenth Street. I don't know the fucking house number though."

"Don't worry," I say slowly. "It will all make sense later. Right now it's confusing and you're scared but later you'll look back and it will be so crystal clear."

"Just let me go."

"Daniel is a biblical name, right?"

"Please...I told you all I know."

"When you go I want...no, I *need* you to walk twenty-three steps into the darkness ahead." I point behind him at the inner courtyard of the school. "Count the steps out and it will make more sense to you. Then, after the twenty-three, you can run, okay."

I can't tell if he gets it at the end of the steps but at least I know he took them. I count every last one and the last I see of him is his dirty black feathers disappearing into the void ahead.

SEVENTEEN

After Daniel leaves, I lay on the cool grass. I feel the wetness of it against my neck and fingertips and I am thankful for this brief moment of peace.

You have such important work to do

I slowly pull myself up from my grave. I am a ghost again. Every night I arise to seek out revenge on those who have killed me. I limp carefully back over to the sidewalk and start towards the light. I should just stay there, in the ground, in the dark. I could sleep a while and feel better but I can't. Not yet.

I feel like rescuing the girl behind the bar before it was too late. She hasn't been wearing those heels for *too* long. There was still time.

I pull open the big front doors of the old stone building and step back inside. A guy and a girl are walking up the stairs from the bar and I see the girl look over at me as she passes. "Hey, are you okay?"She asks.

"I'm fine," I said. "You know what time it is?"

She looks down at her watch before she tells me, "Ten after nine." I say the numbers over in my head but I'm not sure what they mean, if anything. Time is moving too fast for it to be already past nine.

Her boyfriend, or whatever the hell he is, is tugging on

the sleeve of her coat and you can tell he wants to get out of there pretty good. He probably wants to get her home before she changes her mind.

I start down the stairs to the bar. Every step I take seems less real than the last. I can *feel* my grip on this world slipping. I have an hour to live at best. I will have to get a pen and some paper quick so I can tell everyone everything. The best of me in an hour or so.

In front of the entrance to Louis I see three people waiting to get in. A big guy, wearing a 'Louis' t-shirt, stands just inside the bar. He is checking I.D. and it looks like he is being pretty thorough about it.

I wait patiently for my turn. My forehead feels like it's bleeding for some reason and I keep swiping at it with the sleeve of my old army coat. Every time I look down after a swipe I check for blood. I *want* to be bleeding so they might appreciate all I go through. You're tough and you're a survivor it tells everyone. It's easy to be proud of scars on the outside.

"You all right, bud?" The big bouncer asks. He has a shaved head and looks to outweigh me by about a thousand pounds. I get intimidated easily around really big guys and I don't know why. When I was young, maybe my first and second years of school, we had this asshole principal named Mr. Terris. He was a pretty big guy, or at least I remember him being big, and he used to scare the shit out of me. I saw him yelling at another student once, an older kid maybe Grade Six or Seven. Anyway, after I saw him yelling at the kid, I was terrified of old Mr. Terris. I kept thinking I was doing something wrong and that Mr. Terris was going to come and yell at me. I couldn't tie my shoes yet like some of the other kids and that meant Mr. Terris was going to chew me out.

My room was dirty? Here comes Mr. Terris. I lived in constant fear of this guy and looking back I bet he never said two words to me. My mom caught me crying one time and asked me what was wrong. I made the mistake of telling her I was afraid of Mr. Terris and that made her scared of him too. She said, "He has the devil in him." All that did was make me more scared of the poor bastard. You really do have to be careful what you do and say around kids. That's not bullshit. They're watching and if they're like me, then they're watching everything all the time. You can really do a number on them upstairs if you're not careful. Then one day they will find themselves intimidated by a bouncer in a university bar.

"Yeah, I'm okay," I say. "I just wanted to come in for a few."

The bouncer looks behind me and back up the stairs as he says, "You alone tonight?"

"Yes."

"Are you meeting people?"

"What do you mean?"

"You look a little unsteady. Sure you don't have somewhere else more important to be?"

I make eye contact with him and ask him to repeat himself.

You have somewhere else more important to be

"Just wondered if maybe the bar wasn't the place for you tonight, kid. Maybe you had someplace else more important to be, is all."

"Okay. I just...I just got to come in here for a while and relax for a second before I can do anything."

"Can't let you do that, bud."

"Why not?"

"How old are you?"

"Just take care of the girl with the high heels," I say quietly. "I don't think she's supposed to be in there."

"Which girl?"

Another huge monkey in a black 'Louis' t-shirt comes over and starts talking to the first bouncer. I can't hear them too clearly over the music but they keep glancing over at me.

"How's it going tonight?" The second bouncer said, patting me on the shoulder. "Do you need some help, maybe?"

"No...listen, can I..."

"Just walk him over there," the first bouncer said to the second. "It covers are ass because he was in here."

"Take me over where?"

The first bouncer looks at me carefully. I see his eyes come to rest on some of the army patches on my coat. He's wondering about my war wounds. "We're thinking you should go for a little visit over at R.U.H. and get the once over to make sure you're okay."

"The hospital? Why would I need to go to the hospital?" I feel my edges blurring again slightly and I wish I had another drink.

"Just run him over there. It will take you five minutes."

"No," I cut in. "I mean, I'll go or whatever, but let me in for a second so I can calm down and think a little. I sort of really need to talk to the high heel girl."

The second bouncer laughs again. "The last thing either of us need is for you to be in here."

"Why can't I just go?" I feel like a little kid talking to them.

"Listen to me." The second bouncer grabs me by the shoulder and gives me a little shake. "You're mumbling and stumbling around out here, your eyes are as wide as saucers, and you think you need a drink instead of a hospital. That's why you're going."

He doesn't know what is best for me. He doesn't even know me. If he did, he would give me a few on the house and sit and talk to me for a while. Pricks never want to talk to you when you feel like talking.

"Let's go, bud." The first bouncer rests his hand on my coat and starts walking me back up the stairs. I really don't know why I'm following him. I mean, it's not like I *have* to. For some reason, I don't mind. It feels okay with him right now.

I am shivering like a bastard as soon as we step outside but I'm not cold. I'm hot. My body is covered in sweat and my head is itching terribly. I reach up to scratch it and as I do, I lose my balance. The weakness in my legs travels up to my stomach and I feel my insides shift. My mouth instantly fills with saliva and I know I am going to puke. I collapse to my knees and let the puke fly out of me. Foamy beer puke. I check for blood in my vomit but there is none. I want there to be, so people will take me seriously, but there's none.

"You okay?"

"Yes." I run my finger through my hair, combing it off my face. I stand up on my shaky legs and surprisingly, I feel better. Not great or anything, but better. I always puke when I drink tap beer.

We walk together in front of the bus stop where I had first met Daniel. I look up to the library windows and wish so badly I was curled up in one of the cubicles on the floor of twenty-three. Maybe there was another way this could all go down and I don't have to do what I had set out to do.

You don't understand the importance of it all

"You know where you are?"

"Yeah. We're going to the hospital because you think I'm on drugs or something."

"I don't know, man. Something's wrong."

There is no use arguing with him. I don't have the energy to argue anyway. I just keep my mouth shut and continue to walk. I'm on my way to Eighteenth Street to end the world.

Bouncer pulls out a pack of cigarettes from his jeans.

"Can I have one of those?"

He takes a smoke out and holds it in front of me. "So where were you headed tonight?"

"Not sure," I say, taking the smoke and slipping it into the front pocket of my army coat. I look over at bouncer and try to catch his eyes as we walk so he knows I appreciate the damn smoke. People never appreciate anything anymore.

"Well, where did you come from?"

"I was in the Law Library. Just studying, I guess."

"You're a Law student?" He said it like me being a Law student was just about the craziest thing possible.

"Yeah, what's wrong with that?"

"Nothing. You just look a little young is all."

"I'm twenty-four," I said. I'm a terrible liar sometimes.

We walk past the med school building and I regret not saying I am a med student instead. I could've made an excellent med student, if I had ever chosen that field.. I wouldn't bullshit people. I'd tell them exactly how it is. If a guy has a few weeks left to live, then I'd tell him straight up. I wouldn't sit and drag things on for months. I'd be pulling plugs left and right. Doctor Death. That's what they would call me.

"You seem a little rattled. Something happen up there in the library?"

"I told my older brother I was dropping out. I'm going back to the military so I can be a part of something real for once. The law is just pretend, you know. It doesn't even exist."

Bouncer is looking at me like I am a lost cause. Serious mental trauma. Pull the plug.

"What do you mean?"

"The law is there to make things right. Sometimes you have to break the law in order to make things right. It goes against itself."

Bouncer takes a drag on his cigarette like a pro. "So your bro didn't like your little take on the law?

"He told me that the law was the only thing real and that the military was bending the truth. He doesn't even have any *scars* and he's telling me this. Can you believe that?"

Bouncer doesn't say anything. I want him to talk because every time it's quiet I start to get nervous. Panic is creeping around my edges but it's not too bad just yet. It's calling to me and letting me know it's there and that it can have me any time it wants. I think it likes this part the best. The part right before.

"You have some family or somebody I can call to let them know where you are?"

I think he's a nice guy. I can tell. I wouldn't have helped a guy like me if he came stumbling into my bar. I don't trust people enough to help them.

"You could call my brother," I said. My thoughts are racing in my head so fast that I can only catch glimpses of them. Tiny flickers of thought.

"Okay, what's his number?"

I feel my heart pounding through my coat and the tips of my fingers are going numb. It isn't even cold out and my damn fingers are going numb. I feel around in my pocket, hoping that I have another can of booze in my pocket.

"Hey, is there booze? Is there a liquor store around here?" I look over at Bouncer and watch as he kicks a small stone down the street. Going for a little walk while we kick some stones. Afterward, we're going to smash some forts out in the bushes.

Bouncer slows his pace and walks beside me. He grabs a hold of my coat and I think he thinks he is holding me up or something. I am fine. I really am. "Your brother," Bouncer said. "I was going to call your brother for you. Focus buddy."

"My brother? My brother is dead. He killed himself in his car. Everyone knows that." I sort of laugh a little and I think I'm freaked him out or something. I don't know if he thinks I am serious or just joking around with him but he looks pretty concerned about everything.

"It's a good thing the hospital is right next to the University," I said. "I bet that they planned it that way. I wonder if they were thinking about school shootings. I mean, if there was a school shooting, they could save a hell of a lot more people because the hospital is right beside the school, you know. Fuck, with the way the world is going they should just put all the classrooms right in the bloody hospital. High school right in the middle of the psych ward. Wouldn't be much difference, in my opinion." I think I'm just talking so I don't hear anything else. So I won't hear the whispering anymore or have to see all my thoughts flying through my head. It gives me something to focus on. That's all a guy needs when his mirror is broken and his edges are jagged. Something to focus on. A drink. A single thought. The sound of your own voice. Anything really.

I'm not really paying attention to my surroundings to well because suddenly I find myself back under fluorescent light. I've been here before. The ambulance bay right next to the emergency room at Royal University Hospital. I kneel down and feel my knee brush the cold pavement that luckily has no memory.

"You okay, kid?" Bouncer leans down beside me and is patting my back. "Are you going to puke again?"

I lie and tell him I'm going to throw up but I'm fine. I'm not going to puke anymore because all the foamy beer has already come and gone. "I just...I just need a second."

"Okay. We're right outside the emergency room."

I wish I had a head injury so they could actually check me out. If a guy has a head injury, people think he's dead for sure on account of all the blood. Heads bleed a lot. The problem is that the *real* damage happens inside, and you can't see it at first look. They wipe off all the blood and maybe you have a scar or two, but the real damage is all inside. In your brain. That's the stuff that'll kill a guy. Not the blood on your front cover.

I watch as Bouncer walks towards the automatic doors of the emergency room. "Wait. I'll go in on my own. Just give me one second," I call.

Bouncer walks back to me. His footsteps echo inside the empty ambulance bay.

"Thanks a lot for taking me here but I need to go in on my own," I smile. "I mean, I have to maintain at least some dignity here. At least let me walk in on my own."

The bouncer looks me up and down. I think he's really debating whether or not to leave me to my own devices.

"C'mon, man. I'm right outside the bloody doors, I'll be fine. I played football. No one wants to be carried off the field, right? They want to walk off themselves. Even when both their legs are broke and their bleeding from both ears, they want to walk off the field themselves." I should have received a bloody award for that acting, I really should have.

Bouncer looks back over his shoulder towards the emergency room, as if someone will come out and make his decision for him. I stand up to show him that I'll be okay.

"You sure?"

"Yeah, I'm fine. Listen though, I need your number. I'm sure once I get myself together I'm going to want to contact you to thank you." I had never really asked for a number before and it felt strange and awkward doing it.

The bouncer hesitates again before he reaches into his back pocket and pulls out his wallet. He takes out one of the bar business cards and puts it into my hands before saying, "You better stay here. Get yourself looked at."

I think about his words and wonder what some doctor could ever even do with me now.

I walk towards the sliding doors of the emergency room before Bouncer can change his mind and stay with me. Everything has to look like it is in complete control or he will stick around and fuck up everything.

The doors whoosh open and I quickly walk in.

Directly inside, to the right, is a waiting room. I slept there a few nights last year. It's sort of the perfect place to sleep sometimes if you're stuck in the city and have no place to go. No one will bother you there. No one will ask you what you're doing and why you're there. They assume you're waiting for a loved one or something.

I wondered how long I could actually stay there before someone would kick me out.

There is a line-up waiting to register at the front desk and no one notices me come in. I walk straight into the waiting room and head towards the washroom. The door closes heavily and with my sleeve, I turn the lock on the door.

Above the toilet a picture hangs. It is of a magpie perched on a leafless branch. His chest is puffed out and his tail feathers are long and straight. There is no treasure in his beak. He balances so carefully on that branch. One wrong step either way and he will fall. So he chooses not to move. He just sits there wishing for a cigarette and a reason. I wish I could steal that painting.

EIGHTEEN

Everything is a little hazy. My breathing is quick and shallow and no matter how much air I take in, I can't fill my lungs. The waiting room washroom is pretty small and it's making me feel uncomfortable. It feels like another prison cell. I watch myself from behind the glass.

Eighteenth Street

I try and think what my eighteen year will look like but I catch nothing in the whispers to help me. One and eight is nine and I search through my memories for a sign in my ninth year.

Grade Three.

There was a boy in my class named Mark. If I remember right he was from out east somewhere and that was his first and only year at that school. He had an older brother too, like me, and I think that's how we got to talking. One day we end up at his house after school. He was trying to show off a bit and is giving me a little tour of his brother's bedroom and some of his stuff.

His brother had a pellet gun and I remember thinking it was pretty cool to hold that little rifle in my hands. We didn't have any guns or anything at my house so I didn't know a whole lot about them. Mark wanted to take it outside and try it out. Neither of us had ever shot anything before so we figured we'd do it together. At first we just shot at cans and little plastic army men that we lined up against the garage wall but soon Mark dared me to take a few shots at the birds that we're watching along the fence. I never wanted to shoot at anything alive and the thought of it made me sick. Mark was watching though and it changes things when there is an audience.

They were magpies. Big, and black, and cawing like assholes on that fence. They're smart though and it's like they *knew* we were aiming at them because as soon as I'd line one up, he'd fly away and the pellet would zing past him. Mark never knew that I never had any intention of shooting them anyway. I made sure to always keep my aim just a little off so I'd never actually hit them. I think Mark must have been doing the same thing as well because his pellets never hit a damn thing either. We both never wanted to hurt a thing.

On the way back to the house a robin had landed on the edge of the garage. Right at the peak where the two sides of the roof met. He was sitting up there with his bright red chest, singing a song about how bloody great life was or something, I'm sure. Now I swear I didn't even *aim*. All I did was tilt the gun up towards him and fire. The bullet catches him somewhere in his beautiful red chest and he crumples to the ground, as still and silent in death as he was in his last moments of life. It was a weak gun and the poor robin wasn't even killed instantly. He was laying there twitching and trying to flap his wings. His beak was moving up and down and up and down like he was trying to get a last word out.

I started crying and so did Mark. I dropped the gun and ran home. I didn't want to kill it. I never wanted to hurt anything in my entire life. I remember burying my face in my mom's chest and telling her how I wished it had been one of the magpies. Not the happy singing robin. Why couldn't it have been the dirty magpie?

I didn't hang out with Mark much after that and at the end of the year he moved away. Sometimes I wonder if he ever thinks of that robin or the magpies watching. I hope he does. No one likes to be alone with the things that hurt.

This is all I really remember about my ninth year for now. There is nothing there to search for amongst the dirt and grime.

You will feel bad for all of the important work you do
"I know."

One and eight is nine and one and eight is nine and one and eight is nine

I quickly step out of the washroom and shut the door behind me. I look around the waiting room at all the other people. There are seven people waiting. Slow night, I think. Most of them don't look too bad and I wondered if they are just looking for a place to sleep. I think if I would have had a drink with me, I would have stayed and talked with a few of them. You might think that people in emergency rooms wouldn't want to talk but that's not true. A lot of them like to talk. Some of them *need* to talk. You find out which ones need to talk right away. It helps to keep their mind off things, I guess.

I don't know if it's true or not, but I heard that they keep booze in hospitals for people that are coming off of alcohol. I guess if you're a really bad alcoholic, and the booze has eaten away at you for a while, you can't recover when the alcohol is leaving your body so quickly. Your blood pressure shoots up, heart rate sky-rockets, all sorts of shit happen to your kidneys and liver. If you're old enough and in bad enough shape, you die. More people die withdrawing off of alcohol than they do hard drugs. A lot of people don't know that. I think about going up to the front desk and asking for a little nip. I doubt they'd let me have one just to talk with a few sick patients. If I ran a hospital, I'd give booze out all the time. Booze to the mental patients, booze to the sick and dying, booze to the people waiting to hear on loved ones. You might die, but at least you'd die good and plastered, I'd tell them. Doctor Booze. Pull the plug.

No one here could save me tonight. No use wasting their time when someone else, someone who really needed help, was dying in the waiting room. I'll be fine on my own.

I see a few nurses, or whatever the hell they are, sitting behind the registration desk. They are watching me standing here. I feel like I should at least go over there and explain that I am fine. I stop myself before I do. I always feel like I owe people something. That I need to explain every little thing I do. I must have said, "I'm sorry," damn near ten million times in my life. I don't owe anybody anything. Nobody does. It's too bad it takes a guy his whole life to figure that out sometimes. Nobody owes anything to anyone.

The emergency room doors swoosh open again and I walk back into the ambulance bay. Lucky for me there isn't any actual ambulances in there at the moment. I can't stand that sort of thing. The broken and twisted bodies of accident victims being wheeled in to the hospital even though everyone involved knows it's already too late. A doctor still has to try to save them anyway because they have to do *something*, they can't just stand there. The victims bother me, but the family of the victims *really* bother me. I'd rather wade through a thousand dead or dying then have to be around a grieving family. People don't know what to say to a group like that but they feel like they have to say *something*. People say things like, "don't worry, you're going to be okay." Shit like that. They don't know that it will all be okay. They can't see what's inside. They may *never* see the scars inside. Tears dry and people get good at hiding things, but you can't hide what's inside from yourself. Maybe for a while, but not for too long. That's why people shouldn't say, "Everything is going to be okay." They shouldn't say anything at all. Just keep quiet and stand there. Your presence is enough to show you care.

To my right is a door that has been propped open with a mop bucket. I walk towards the door, being careful not to drag my coat or jeans over top of that dirty old mop bucket. I'd have to toss my clothes and walk home in my underwear if that happened.

The cool nighttime air feels good on my face. I stand there for a second and let the breeze blow into me. I can smell the river in the distance and the scent of diesel left over from some earlier ambulance. It calms me for a second and I can think. I can actually reach out and hold on to a thought instead of having it flicker and pop inside my head before disappearing.

"Nice night, isn't it?"

A man steps out from the other side of the ambulance bay. He looks about forty and is dressed in dark clothes. A vest across his chest reads 'SECURITY'. A walkie-talkie hangs from his belt. He has stepped outside for a smoke. I can see the end of the little cancer stick burning and I remember the smoke I have in my pocket.

Security walks over to me as I say, "Yeah, really nice night. Not too many of these left before winter." That's what people do when they talk to strangers. You talk about the weather and silently give thanks you have a cigarette to kill the silence between questions.

"How's it going tonight?" he asks, taking a short drag on his cigarette before knocking the butt off perfectly with his index finger. A real pro. Probably die of lung cancer by the time he was sixty. Maybe they would even wheel him into the hospital through the very doors he protected when he was a working stiff.

"Not too bad. I took a wrong turn though." I motion to the bay behind me. "Didn't realize this was the emergency."

"What are you looking for?"

"The liquor store, actually. Any around here?"

The security guard takes another drag. He smiles and says, "Not around here. I guess downtown would be the closest place."

"Downtown." I try to picture how far of a walk that will be. It was only down the University Bridge and then a couple of blocks.

"Know the city well?"

"No. I'm in on business. Taking care of some shit a junior guy screwed up. Went and ordered about a thousand wrong parts for this huge customer of ours. Punks these days." I shook my head like I was really pissed about it.

"Sounds bad. What type of business is that?"

I can feel myself sort of breaking up a little and I don't feel like talking all that much. My legs are shaking and I can't get my breath in deep enough again. It's like I have swallowed a bunch of concrete or something and it's now travelling through my blood stream. The security guard is talking but I can't make out what he's saying. Everything feels lost in translation before it ever make any sense to me. I just want him to be quiet. I need him to stop talking so I can think in the silence for a bit.

"I'm sorry. I can't hear what you're saying. My ears were damaged in combat." I've cut him off mid-sentence but I don't care.

He looks at me carefully before answering, "Don't worry about it."

"A shell landed near me in Iraq," I shake the little badge on my coat towards him. "I'm damn lucky I made it out alive."

Security sort of nods at me, his cigarette held awkwardly in his hand.

"Nice talking with you," I smile at him for some reason because that's what people do.

I start walking in the direction of the University Bridge. Behind me, I can hear Security saying something else but I don't turn around. It's taking everything I have just to keep my feet moving forward towards the bridge. I close my eyes and try to concentrate on the feeling of my feet as they glide over the pavement of the sidewalk.

I look around as I walk. Everything is silent. No cars, no people, just me and the sound of the wind blowing off of the river.

I wonder how cold the water is and if the river has a memory.

You can't just stand outside of places

The whispers of the river are getting louder the closer I get to the bridge. The water rushes by underneath and I stop walking so I can make out the words within its language.

I step on to the bridge and start walking. My breathing

feels better here. It's deeper and more comfortable. Maybe it's the river but I don't know.

The Bessborough is lit up and looks like something out of a fairy tale. The Bessbourough is this old hotel that sits on the river bank and the damn thing looks like a castle, honestly it does. As a kid, any time I heard a story about some damn King or Queen, I figured they must have lived at the Bess. Probably a lot of kids like me in Saskatoon. It's not just the hotel though. There are tons of other beautiful buildings down here by the river. You'd think Saskatoon was the most beautiful city in the world if you walked down this bridge at the right time of day. They call Saskatoon the 'Paris of the Prairies'.

That's the thing about Saskatoon. It's a great looking city sometimes. Deceptive in a way because you get caught up in how good it looks and forget about all the bad things inside. I look out at those buildings and wonder how many husbands are cheating on their wives in one of the hotel rooms. Maybe there's a drug deal going on in one of the apartments. At this time of night, there was probably about a million drunk people getting in fights and scaring their children. There could be rapes and murders and stabbings going on the whole time you are staring at this postcard view of the city. It makes me hate it. It looks good on the outside and it should look bad. It was just like one big magpie nest lined with tinsel and shiny things. So shiny that you forget all about everything else that doesn't shine.

I wish I could just stop thinking about all of this and just enjoy the damn view for once like everyone else.

If I ever find myself with a whole bunch of money I'd like to start buying up the city. I would buy the Bess and then slowly start buying up all the condos and apartments, the churches, everything eventually. I wouldn't live in anything because that would defeat the whole purpose. I'll keep everything empty and clean. Once I kick everyone out there might be a little fuss but I won't let it bother me because no one would be able to understand all the important work I was doing. I'll just continue my work and go on building my perfect city. I'll make sure all of downtown is completely empty. Not one person. Except for street sweeping and the odd janitorial work, no one will ever step foot in the new downtown Saskatoon. It will be empty and quiet. Perfect and clean. As it was meant to be. I would love to walk up and down the University Bridge and admire the downtown view then. It wouldn't be ruined anymore. The thought of all the bad things going on won't be there to bother me. I could finally see what everyone else sees and be happy.

Up ahead the bridge is ending and I have to make a choice about which direction to go. I could keep heading straight and go further downtown or I could turn left. There's a real nice pathway along the river called the Meewasin Trail and if I turn left I can walk it for a while. Sometimes, in the summer, I fill up a water bottle with some booze and pop and go walking along the trail. It's not too bad if you can walk it alone and everything but it sort of gets a little depressing when you keep running into about a thousand people out for a walk or something. It's weird. You pass these people, just for a tiny bit of time, a few seconds maybe, and they make you feel like a real piece of shit. They might look really happy, walking with a friend or loved one and it makes you feel so damn lonely you could shoot yourself. Or sometimes, someone is running down the trail, alone, and you feel bad for them because they're just going to die anyway no matter how far they run. Fuck, I even got depressed one time because I saw an old guy walking his dog. Just him and his dog. It made me so depressed I had tears running down my face and I damn near dropped my liquor bottle. I was thinking that maybe he had a wife at one time but she kicked off a few years ago. Cancer. They had planned on having kids but it never really worked out and eventually it was too late. He was so damn old that all of his friends had died too. All the sad old bugger had was that stupid dog. Both of them hoping they'd go first so they wouldn't die alone. For all I *really* knew, the old man's wife was at home playing with their hundred or so grandkids maybe. I couldn't know for *sure* though, so it bothered me so bad I had to stop walking that day. Now, whenever I feel like going for a walk down the trail, I try to find a part of the trail that's empty. I may not get to walk very far but it beats the hell out of getting so depressed you could take a bath with a toaster.

I decide I don't feel like walking the trail tonight and that I'd rather go straight. I think I would've liked to go left but I can't think of any liquor stores that way and I know, for sure, that there is one straight ahead and that it was only four or five blocks.

I pass a hotel. The Parktown, I think it's called. It's pretty nice, I guess, but I don't know that for sure because I've never been in it.

I am looking across the street when I suddenly remember they have an off-sale. A little neon 'OPEN' sign hangs in the darkened window adjacent to University drive. I cross the street and walk up the ramp way to the little store.

I pull open the door and a bell jingles above me, announcing my arrival. A girl, maybe a few years older than me, looks up briefly from the desk ahead. There are a few books opened up beside her, scraps of loose leaf and pens laid out on the flat surface of the check-out counter. A university student. Studying and working so she could grow up and have a happy life and buy the Bess so she can do her drugs in peace and ruin my view.

All the hard alcohol is behind the counter. The rest of the store is devoted to beer. I feel like vodka because I have been drinking it most of the night and I don't feel like changing. People always seem obsessed with going and changing things these days.

I stand in front of the counter and wait for the girl to look up from her textbook. She casually glances up but I can't seem to get the words out. They are trapped inside me and all I can do is point at a bottle of vodka behind her.

"Rough night," she says, grabbing my bottle from off the shelf.

"Yes," I croak.

She eyes me suspiciously. I think she's going to ask me for I.D. but instead she says, "You sure you need this?"

"I don't think it can hurt at this point," I say slowly. "I'll be dead soon anyway."

She runs the vodka under the scanner and places it into a small brown bag. "What do you mean, you'll be dead?

"Cancer." I take the bottle out of the bag and slip it into my jacket. "We all have cancer and there's nothing we can do about it."

The girl hands me my change and as she does I notice her arms. There are four thin scars running parallel along her wrist. Her forearm has an older mark along its entire length. It is purple and faded and I wonder how deep she would have had to push to cut like that.

"Are you okay?"

I want to answer but she keeps glancing down at her notes and textbook. Her life is so busy and disconnected. There is no time for cancer or suicide or magpies.

"What are you going to be?" I finally say to break such an uncomfortable silence. "Like, when you grow up and you've read all the books, what are you going to be?"

"I don't know," she said slowly. "I'm just in school because I don't know what else to do."

I'm so glad that she told me the truth. The truth is so rare in my life that when I *do* hear it, it takes me a second to realize that it isn't a lie. Cutter girl could have told me some bullshit like she was going to be a psychologist or an accountant or something. Something that you're supposed to say so people think you're doing something with your time. Instead, she told me the truth. She doesn't know. Nobody knows.

Cutter girl's cancer is in remission.

"That's good," I say.

Cutter girl shifts uncomfortably behind the counter. She really wants me to leave, I can tell. I wish she wanted to talk but it is probably a bad idea anyway. She might end up saying something that takes away her shine and I don't want to deal with that right now.

"Take care of yourself," she says as I move towards the door.

I walk out of the store and the little bell above me jingles. I am barely down the ramp before my hand moves into my coat pocket and pulls out the smooth plastic bottle. I twist the top off and the sharp smell of vodka hits my nose. I take a small sip. The vodka burns in my throat but soon finds a comfortable home somewhere deep inside of me.

I start my trek down University Drive. It's a nice little street and every time I go down it, it reminds me of my childhood. One of uncles lived in this big apartment just off of this street. I remember thinking he must have been a millionaire or something. He lived near the top floor of the apartment. I mean, the higher your bird nest was, the more tinsel you must have, is how I saw it at the time. He died a few years back. Cancer. Like everyone else. It doesn't matter if you're a millionaire when you have cancer.

I see Kinsmen Park to my right. A big park right in the middle of the city. They have this Ferris wheel and merry-go-round and water park. It's a blast when you're a kid and don't know any better. You can buy tickets and ride this little train they have all around the entire park. I guess it would be about ten or so cars long where you could sit with all the people who loved you and didn't let you know how bad things would get when you got off that train for the last time. I loved going on that train but there was always a bunch of assholes that ruined it for me every time. There was a tunnel the train went through and it was dark as hell. Anyway, the rest of the kids would yell, no *scream*, every time we went through that damn tunnel and it used to scare the hell out of me. When I have money I'm going to buy that entire place and rip down that tunnel. I'll keep the train though. I have no problem with the train. I'll be the conductor and I'll let all the kids ride for free whenever they want. There is only one rule. They can never get off and they can never yell. I won't be able to protect them any longer the second they step off of the train. It will be up to them, of course. They have to choose.

On my left, across from Kinsmen Park, is a funeral

parlor. Where we said goodbye to my mom. I think there might have been twenty people at her bon voyage. Mostly family. She sort of alienated everyone else in her last few years so it was no big shock that the place was empty. Most people didn't know she was sick. To be honest with you, I couldn't remember a thing about that day. Not one thing. Maybe if I had been a little older. All I could remember about the damn thing was a bunch of candies my brother gave to me. There I was, chewing on these damn candies, and my brother beside me crying his eyes out. It never really bothered me all that much. My mom used to scare me. I don't want to say that I was relieved when she died, but it didn't bother me like it did my dad and brother.

It's not my fault you went and smashed her all over the floor

I look up and somewhere in the tinted black windows of the funeral home my mother watches me. I see her silhouette bends and twists like fog along the river.

"It was an accident," I whisper to her. "I didn't know they would break."

Stole my mind you smashed her all over the floor the devil in him

She is whispering so fast now that I can't make out the words. I move towards the window and the terrible sounds gets louder. I stop walking because I can't stand to hear anymore words in the hissing.

Important work to do

I try to see her more clearly through the window. I strain but I won't take a step closer.

I put my hand in to my pocket and pull out the bottle again. This time my sip is bigger and I gag as it gallops down my throat. I bring the bottle to my mouth once more. I swallow until her whispers fade.

I am across from where I used to ride the trains and go on the Ferris wheel. Just in front of the building where we said goodbye to my mother. Funny the places a guy ends up sometimes.

NINETEEN

There is a 7-11 at the end of the street. In front of it I see my first signs of life on University Drive. Three kids, younger than me, I think. They are milling about by the doors as they smoke cigarettes and wonder what they're doing with their lives.

I am hoping they ignore me but I think they are happy to see someone else alive as well. The war has ravaged our city. Only a few souls remain. The lucky ones or unlucky ones, depending on how you see things. After all, what kind of life is it to scrounge around the broken and decayed buildings as you look for food and tinsel. Trying to survive even though the radiation blast has seared your insides, leaving you with cancer. You won't last long but what else are you to do.

I get like that sometimes. I pretend I'm in a war. Everything is broken and destroyed and somehow I have survived. Not because I'm smarter or stronger or anything like that. It was just luck. Nothing more and nothing less than stupid blind luck. I guess it helps me to make sense of people and the things they do when I pretend it's because of the war.

One of them approaches me. A boy, maybe fifteen or so. He is dressed in baggy jeans and skater shoes and a bright red hoodie. "Bro," he says, glancing over his shoulder. "Think you could score us some smokes?"

I look behind him at his friends who watch us carefully. Their night depends on me because you can't just stand outside of places. You have to have a reason.

Red Hoodie holds out a ten-dollar bill.

"Yeah, I can get you a pack," I say.

I walk in through the glass doors of the 7-11. At the register, an older woman looks up from her magazine. Her mid-length hair is thin and straight and looks like she dyed it herself with a three dollar box of product. She wears no makeup and her hands are stained with tobacco.

I feel her eyes on me as I stroll through this fluorescent feed trough. To my left, chicken in various states waits patiently to be eaten and I wonder if I should buy something to eat. I try to remember the last time I ate. This morning? Yesterday? I don't really know. I don't feel hungry, just numb and empty.

There is music playing from somewhere above me. I close my eyes and listen, trying to figure out what song it is. I don't recognize it. Maybe it's not a song at all but just the air conditioner. It is a quiet steady hum that keeps the old lady at the till alive just enough to turn the pages.

The reason I am in this space has slipped my mind. For a brief moment, I stand here, staring at the bright smooth plastic of everything and hoping I find the reason.

Cigarettes

And like that, I remember.

I walk up to the till and wait for the Till Lady to look down at me from her lofty perch.

"How can I help you?" she says, her voice dry and hoarse from years of smoking.

"Export A, please," I say quickly. I wait for her to ask

me for my identification but for some reason she doesn't. We're both too tired to go through the motions.

Till Lady places the pack of cigarettes down on the counter and takes the ten bucks from my hand. Her hand quivers and shakes slightly and I wonder if she's an old boozer or just one of the unlucky ones. There are no rings on her fingers and I wonder if she killed her husband through second hand smoke. She feels awfully guilty about the whole thing. They spent every last dime they had trying to cure it. Mexico. Ripped off by some faith-healer who drives a Cadillac and shakes your hand with both of his. He uses chicken guts in his act. The same chicken guts sitting under a heating lamp next to the Till Lady right now. A constant reminder.

"Anything else?" She mumbles.

I hold the pack of cigarettes tightly in my fist. "I want you to have a very nice evening." I say as slow and as clear as I can stand it.

I watch as her eyes slightly brighten like a lit match before slowly fading back to black. She chuckles and says, "You too then."

Outside, I walk back over to the three youth huddling in the dark. For a brief moment, I wonder if they might jump me as soon as I hand over the cigarettes. If they do, I'll shoot them. The thought is there in my mind and there is no use pretending it doesn't exist. After the war, a person could shoot another person for any old reason at all.

"Thanks bro," the boy in the red hoodie says as he walks towards me. His thin face is smiling and I am so thankful I don't have to shoot him. The light from above us allows me to see him more clearly and I notice that he is Native.

"Thank you," I say to him because I'm not sure what else to say.

Behind him, his companions move closer. Another young Native boy in a dark black hoodie. He's shorter than Red Hoodie but stockier. He keeps his hands in his front pockets as he walks so that you can't tell if he's simply keeping his hands warm or getting ready to pull out a knife. It makes you aware of him and I wonder if this is the point.

Beside Black Hoodie is a Native girl in a red long-sleeve t-shirt. She is thin and frail and walks delicately on thin legs like she might trip and smash all over the place. Her long black hair is pulled back in a pony-tail and her smooth face is thin and angular.

Red Hoodie takes the pack from me and calmly opens it. He pulls one out and holds it out towards me. Then, carefully pulling two more out, he hands them to his friends. He only takes one for himself after completing this ritual. Every family has rituals, you know.

"I'm Shay," Red Hoodie says to me. "This is Rob and Janice," he points towards them with his cigarette.

"Have a nice evening," I whisper before turning and walking back towards the store. Before I am five-feet away from them, I pull out my bottle and take another drink. There is more than half left and I hope it will be enough to make it to Eighteenth Street and beyond.

"Hold on, Janice calls to me. "We're going that way too. We'll walk with you."

I wait for them and the thought of them still jumping me crosses my mind. They seem harmless enough but sometimes that's what people want you to believe. You read their cover and dismiss them and they make you pay for it later on. I do it all the time.

They move towards me in unison, like they are one person. I envy their closeness and wonder about the wars they've been through.

When I see that, people that are close to one another, I'm reminded of my brother. I'm reminded that I often fool myself into thinking we were close, but we never really were. Everyone in my family lived in separate houses under one roof. Yet, even though we might not have been as close as I like to think, he still should have taken care of me. He never should have left me alone. My mom was going to go. There was no way we could have stopped that. Sometimes, people can't be helped. Too many things were taking and pulling on her and she needed to go. It would have been like putting together a broken mirror. Its better she's gone. But my brother, he could've lived. All he needed was someone telling him that's he'd be okay. He just needed someone to walk with.

"Where are you going?" I feel Janice brush up against me and I'm not sure if I imagine her voice or actually hear it. My edges are so broken right now and |I sort of have to shift through the shards to make sense of it all.

"You all right, man?" Shay asks me. He squints his eyes and leans towards me like he is examining me in a laboratory somewhere. When his face relaxes, I notice he has a bruise under his eye and a cut along his nose. War wounds.

I breathe in as deeply as I can. 'I'm fine. I'm just headed over to Eighteenth Street. Are you okay? You look like you were in a fight?'

Shay laughs and I notice that neither Janice nor Rob laugh with him. They are silent and sullen like the bruises connect them all. The real injuries are deep and internal and Shay is the lucky one for he only bears the surface wounds.

"He got jumped by some guys," Rob said. He lifts his smoke to his mouth and takes one long drag,

"What goes around comes around." Shay laughs like nothing will ever bother him. We pass under the street light and I can see that his neck is covered in tattoos. It is too dark to make out what they depict. They are just a mess of jumbled colour and I doubt they were done by a professional hand.

Rob finally gives in and laughs with him. Barely anyone ever means it when they laugh anymore.

I look over at Janice. Her shirt is too thin to be walking around out here for long and I wonder how she found herself outside without a coat on. She doesn't act cold though. She acts like the wind blows around her as if she doesn't even exist.

"You look like you've been outside a long time," Rob said.

"No. Not really. I'm just walking around, I guess."

"Dangerous at this time of night."

"I know."

To our left a car passes. For a moment, I am sure it is the Mustang. It's my brother coming to pick me up and take me home so I can sleep. When I look at the taillights though, they are wrong. The car isn't a Mustang. I have no idea what it is, but it's definitely not the Mustang. I hang onto this reality for as long as I can stand it.

"What are you doing out here? I ask.

"We're looking for my little sister," Janice said. "She ran away or something again."

"Fuck," Shay laughs again. I am starting to think he is on something because he is laughing like a jackass at everything. "She's probably out hooking for blow. Isn't that right, Janice?"

"Fuck you, Shay."

"Hey, I'm only out here because I'm supposed to walk you."

"I don't need anyone to walk me," Janice mutters. "Especially some skinny gangster wannabe."

Shay takes a drag on his cigarette and narrows his eyes. "I'm no wannabe."

"Are you in a gang?" I say it quickly because I am curious. It wouldn't be a huge surprise if Shay was in a gang because a lot of the Native kids are in gangs in Saskatoon.

"He *knows* gang members," Janice answers for him.

"Soon enough," Shay said. "I'm a *Stryker*." He spits the word out like it's a weapon carried on the smoke that exits his mouth. He stands here, staring at me, watching for any reaction.

"What's a Stryker?" I indulge him.

"It means he's a dumbass who does what other dumbasses want him to do until he's finally one of them," Janice said. "He's an initiate."

"You should watch your mouth," Shay said. "Talking like that might get a little bitch like you in trouble." He is smiling but I can't tell if he's angry or not. He makes me uncomfortable with his shiftiness and the strange smile that never leaves his face.

"Shay, you talk too much," Rob said. One hand remains in his front pocket as he smokes.

Shay looks back at Rob who has fallen a few steps behind us and nods at him. Then, he shifts over and slides in beside me.

"You looking for anything, bro? A little blow or some

weed maybe. A piece of tail?" Shay reaches over and grabs Janice's ass.

Janice turns quickly and slaps it away. "Fuck off."

Shay laughs before patting Janice's back. "I'm just bugging you."

"I'm good," I said. "I mean, I don't need anything. I have no money because my wallet was stolen." I want them to think I have no money in case they think of robbing me.

"Well, what about the tax we have to charge you?" Shay said, throwing his arm around my shoulder.

"What tax?"

Janice pushes Shay's arm off of my back. "Leave him alone," she said.

"No money means maybe you better give me that bottle," Shay turns quickly and lifts up the front of his jacket. The handle of a small pistol is sticking out of the waistband of his boxers.

My hand grips the bottle in my pocket and I feel my body go cold. I stand still underneath the Saskatoon street light staring at Shay. He doesn't know I have a much bigger gun than him.

"Ha, just fucking with you, bro." Shay bends over and laughs again. He pulls out the gun and takes a shooter's stance. I don't know anything about guns so I can't tell you what kind or anything, but my gun would kill him. He pretends to shoot off three rounds.

This is why I hate people. You never know what they're thinking. They could shoot you or kiss you or both. They're crazy sometimes. I think that eventually I'll get to the point where I never trust anyone again. I'll just stay inside my room all day. Alone and safe.

"Put that away," Janice yells. She looks over at me,

"Don't worry about him, he thinks he's a real big deal now or something."

I feel safe with Janice here. She is like a leash to Shay's pit-bull.

"Where you from, bro?" Shay walks back over to me. I think he thinks he scared me and now he's trying to show me everything is cool.

"Here. Well, around here. You guys?"

"Saskatoon, Prince Albert, North Battleford, Regina. All over the fucking place."

We are right downtown now and the city is asleep. I can see the big auditorium in the distance. I went to my brother's high school grad there. It feels like I haven't been in that auditorium in a thousand years. It has a new name now. I can't remember what it is. Everything's names are always changing and it makes a guy crazy trying to keep up with it all. Corporations are the ones who go and change everything. Money. There should be a rule that once you name something you can't go back and change it again because if you do you're liable to make someone go insane.

We keep walking and this small group surrounds me. Shay is talking but I can't make out what he is saying. I try to count his steps so I can get a hold on him but he's shifty and unpredictable and nothing stays the same. He steps then shuffles then steps again. He's cutting my edges more jagged with every second that passes and it's making me drink too much.

I see myself, alone, in the reflection of the black glass of the auditorium windows. I look strange and wispy, like smoke. I look for the reflection of my three companions but I don't see them. Maybe their shadows are too dark. Maybe they don't even exist.

I take my eyes off the glass and see Janice up ahead. She is walking fast along the sidewalk. She covers ground quickly with tiny little bird steps. Her hands are curled into balls because they are cold. Shay is beside her. They are talking about something I can't hear. She is mad. He is laughing.

It takes everything I have to keep up with them. No matter how fast I try to move my legs, the further and further away they seem to get. It's like they are ghosts. I don't hear the sounds of their shoes on the pavement. I don't hear anything at all.

I have had enough of walking and so I stop. I unscrew the top off the vodka bottle and take a long drink. It burns a little when I swallow and when I bring my head back up, the world shifts violently. I would trade all the money in the world just to go home right now.

"Hey, you okay?" Rob calls to me.

I hear the tiny quick patter of Janice's steps as she hops back to me. I don't open my eyes because my head feels better with them closed. I just stand there, listening to her coming closer. I count her steps and try to find meaning in the sounds.

"Are you okay?"

"Yes. I'm just...I'm just taking a break because my head hurts."

She grabs the sleeve of my coat and I feel her tug on it before she says, "Come over and sit here."

She leads me to a little stone flowerbed or something in front of the YMCA or YWCA, whatever the fuck it is. The one beside the auditorium of a thousand names. She motions for me to sit and so I do.

I open my eyes and watch Shay and Rob walking

towards us. A cigarette dangles perfectly out of the Stryker's mouth. "What's going on?"

"He's taking a break. His head hurts."

"You're pissed, buddy. Should have given me that bottle."

I manage a smile on the outside.

"Give me a drink." Shay said.

I hand over the bottle and say, "You mind if I bum another one of them smokes?"

"I got a joint we can smoke instead, if you want that?" He takes a small sip from the bottle and hands it back. I don't think he drinks very often.

"No, I don't think so. Just a regular smoke would be good."

He passes over the cigarette. "I won't even bother asking you to smoke a joint." He kicks playfully at Janice's feet.

"I don't do drugs."

"No, that's cause your sister does them all before you get a chance to," Shay laughs and even Rob joins him.

Janice is quiet and I can see that she is shivering. I feel like I'm in damn sauna or something. I slip my coat off of my shoulder and say, "Take my coat. I'm so hot I could puke."

"No, it's fine."

"Seriously. I'm taking it off anyway because I'm so hot. You might as well wear it." I wasn't really going to take it off but she doesn't know that. I'd rather be cold for a while anyway. Change things so I feel better.

Janice lights my cigarette for me and I inhale. The quick intake of smoke is too much for me and I cough. "I don't want this." Janice thinks I'm talking about the cigarette and she takes it from me.

I sip again at my bottle. It is the only thing around me that feels real. Nothing else feels real at all.

"What's on Eighteenth?" Shay says to me as a little grey tendril of smoke rises from the end of his cigarette.

I look at him carefully. "I'm looking for a guy. Faran Bird. Someone told me he lives over there."

Janice pulls on my coat. It looks like a big blanket on her. It covers and shields her completely and I think we are both glad for this fact even if it leaves me out in the cold. "We know who that is," she said softly.

"Why are you looking for him?" Rob asks. He finally pulls his hands out of his pockets and I'm relieved to see they are empty. "You probably shouldn't go messing with the Bird man, you know."

The bird man

"He knows my brother well," I say. "I'm *supposed* to go see him.

Shay kicks at a small chunk of gravel that lies on the street. We listen as it echoes down the cold hard pavement before coming to a rest somewhere near the auditorium. "You looking for drugs? Any man looking for Faran is looking for drugs," he says calmly. The laughter is gone from his voice and I notice he is staring hard at me.

"I'm…I'm not looking for drugs," I manage to say. "My brother said to go see him and that Faran would be expecting me."

Rob looks over at Shay. "He doesn't live on Eighteenth," he said. "Where's he stay, man? You know."

Shay shoots a cold glance toward Rob. "How the fuck should I know? I'm not the man's keeper. Ask the sister of his biggest customer." He waves his cigarette at Janice who looks like she'd like nothing more than to disappear deeper into my old jacket.

"He doesn't live on Eighteenth but he comes by there often," Janice said to me. "I think he lives over on Twenty-Third but I don't know."

"You live on Eighteenth?" I ask.

I wonder what my eighteenth year will look like and whether or not I will wake up on that day. My years twist and curve, the paths dirty and littered with trash. Magpies block the way. They are too busy stuffing their beaks with the garbage and filth of my life in the hopes they might consume something shiny. Some might find something. Most won't. It's those birds that will choke to death along my path and it will take all I have to wade through their dead bodies.

"Yeah, there's a few of us living in a house over there. I'll take you and see if anyone has seen Faran."

You have important work to do

I hope for another outcome. That something will happen and there can be another way to get through this but I know this can't be. There are many paths but they all lead to this doorway. I feel the gun against my stomach and wonder if I'll even be able to pull the trigger. In a way, I think I already have.

"I can't stay out here all night long, Janice. You have to decide where you're going." Shay keeps kicking at Janice's feet and I wonder if the guy has ever sat still in his whole damn life. He is shiftless and jagged and never at peace. Like a leaf blowing in the wind.

"Just go then."

"Well, where are you going?"

"Don't worry about it, Shay. Just go."

Shay looks unsure of his next moves. He shifts from one foot to the other. "Well, you catch up with me tomorrow and I'll ask around about your sister." He looks over at me. "Or maybe I'll stop by later."

"Whatever."

Shay kicks at Rob's foot. "You coming with me or them?"

"Where are you going?"

"I don't know," Shay replies.

Shay gives me one last look before he turns and starts walking up the street. Rob follows after him without saying goodbye because it's easier to be there one minute and gone the next.

I listen to the sounds of their feet as they bounce along the cold pavement until I can't hear them anymore and the city became silent as a tomb once again.

TWENTY

We sit on the bench and wait for Janice to finish her cigarette. There are no sounds at all except for when she exhales and I'm glad for the silence. I think we're both happy just to have everything lay silent for a while. It's the calm before a storm that you are powerless to stop. When I finally get home after all of this, I plan on climbing into bed and not hearing anything for at least a hundred years or so. I will lie there in the silence like I'm dead.

"You okay to go now?"

I look up. Janice is watching me. She has pulled my big coat tightly around her and she's no longer shivering. It is only then that I notice a breeze blowing and that I am cold. I take another sip and say, "Yeah. I guess we can't sit out here all night."

We stand up and it feels like my legs are going to fall off. Like they can't wait any longer. They've died before the rest of me could. I shake them to wake them up.

"So, you're sure you want to head over to Eighteenth?" She coughs after she speaks and I think of the tobacco chemicals responsible and the men responsible for those chemicals.

I think about her question for a while before I answer "I think that's where I need to be."

We start walking towards Idywyld Drive and it is right about then that I can hear Janice humming that damn tune. It's very subtle and she doesn't even do it all the time, just when I stop watching her.

"What are you looking at?" She asks.

"What's that song you're humming? It's familiar, like it's right on the tip of my tongue but I can't make it out."

"I'm not humming," she smiles and I notice how tight the skin is on her thin face.

"Sure you are. Are you embarrassed or something?"

Janice stops walking and grabs my arms. She pulls me closer and then peers into my eyes. Two little dark pools of oil darting back and forth from one eye to the other like she can't tell which one is telling her the truth. "Are you sure you're okay? I'm not humming anything."

My mouth opens to protest but I catch myself. I see her looking at me and I get it. We shouldn't be talking about it so deep in enemy territory. The answer will always be the same no matter how many times I ask.

I'm not humming

"How drunk are you?" There is no disgust in her tone. I think it is just a question and nothing more.

"I'm fine," I reply. I'm not wasted or anything, but I have to be careful with every step and watch where I am going. Everything is blurring around my edges and if I'm not careful I'll fall over and smash all over the road. I use the telephone poles as markers. I do my best to focus on them, one at a time. All I have to do is make it to the next pole. Life is simple sometimes.

Janice walks beside me with her little silent steps. My coat looks funny on her, the arms hanging down damn near to her knees but I don't think she minds. We're in the same platoon.

"My cousin rents the house on Eighteenth. Sometimes I stay there. I'm going to check and see if Justine has been around and if I don't find her, I'll sleep for the night."

"Justine is your sister?"

"Yes."

"You think she's in trouble?" I should just leave everything alone. Sometimes people don't want to talk about things and the worst thing you can do is try and make them. You have to wait until they're ready and be prepared for the fact that maybe they never will be.

"I don't know. She's a little messed up with drugs and everything. Her friends are idiots."

"I hate drugs." I said.

I think of my brother. Afterward, they called him a drug addict. I don't know if that's *really* true because it wasn't like he was using them around me or something. Of course, people can't accept things and they always start looking for reasons. There has to be a *reason*. So maybe it is just easier to dismiss him as a drug addict. It is the reason and in the end you can't do a damn thing to change it anyway so take that reason and run. It took so long to get any real information anyway. The information had to be sifted through. It had to be pieced together and every thread unraveled. They don't tell you everything when you're just a kid.

We're having a war against the Grade Sixes

I'd buy all the drugs in the world, if I could. One big deal. Then I would flush them all down the toilet. I would devote my life to it. I would sit on some dirty floor of a bathroom somewhere, slowly pouring out packets of coke and meth and oxy and heroin and whatever into the toilet. It will take me thousands and thousands of years to do it because there are so many bad people out there. I'll have to drink a hell of a lot of booze to get through it because of how depressed it makes me. I'll think about all the people and what they had wanted to be when they grew up. Finally, when I am done, I can pour out the booze into the toilet too. It will all be gone and I'll flush the toilet. Unfortunately, it might not change anything. Once the drugs are gone, it's the people who will have to be dealt with.

"She thinks her friends are the only ones who understand. It's like she couldn't survive without them and their influence. I keep telling her I've been through it too but she doesn't want to listen."

"People never listen when you have something important to say."

"She's working the streets now and the funny thing is that she's doing it as a way to keep some control over her life. At least she has some money and doesn't have to beg some dealer for it, is how she sees it."

I don't say anything. I hope she won't tell me details about Justine because all it will do is depress the shit out of me. I already have enough things trapped in my mind and if I hear something like this about some poor little bird, I'll sit and think about it for the rest of my life. I will wonder what happened and how her story ends. I'll probably have to go out and get a license and patrol the streets, protecting her from the johns or something. The less I know the better.

"She just doesn't see."

"But you don't do that anymore, right? I mean, you're okay." I need her to be okay. The whole damn world couldn't be fucked up, could it? At least *someone* has to be okay.

I slip my bottle of liquor out and take two swallows because I am afraid of what she might say.

"I still run with the same people but I don't do all the stupid stuff like when I was younger. I don't have to. No one owns me or anything. They're like family and you can't just leave family so easily."

"Is Faran Bird part of your family?" I try to say it as calmly as I can stand it.

"No, not really. He's older and one of those guys that everyone just sort of knows, I guess. He hangs around a few of my cousins. Gang stuff."

I am silent as we walk, playing scenarios over in my mind. The gun feels heavy and cold against my skin and a part of me wants to throw it in the river.

"You have a problem with Faran?" She looks over at me.

"I need to see him for my brother. I guess he got some bad stuff off of him. Faran was going to fix it."

She's humming again but this time I don't say anything about it.

"Well, do what you have to do, I guess."

"What did you say?" I turn and try to look at her face but her focus is on the road ahead.

"Do what you have to do." She says again.

Do what you have to do because you have such important work to do what you have to do

I close my eyes to stop the rush of voices. Among them, I hear Janice but I won't bother asking her to repeat it. She has her own set of voices to deal with.

I stop walking once more so that I can unscrew the cap off of my bottle of vodka. I take a short drink and moments later I feel it hit my guts. It hurts. Burns in a way that I'm not used to. Maybe I've burned a hole in my stomach because I always forget to eat.

Janice looks back at me and stops walking. The streetlights overhead light up her hair and face and I think how pretty she will be.

I walk towards her as quickly as I can manage. "Sometimes I wish I could start again somewhere. With a new face and name. Do you ever feel like that? Do you ever feel like going out west and signing up for some classes or something?"

Janice doesn't answer. Instead, she slips off my coat. "Here, put this back on."

"No, you keep it. I'm fine."

"No you're not. You're shivering all over the place. Put it on. If you're such a gentleman, we can share it. We'll trade off with it every few blocks."

It is true. I am shivering like a wet dog but I don't think it is because I am cold. I take back the coat anyway and pull it on.

A wind has picked up, blowing cool fall air in from off the river. It blows through downtown and finally finds Janice and me as we walk through the sleeping city. It's strange, but you never realize how cold you can get until you're finally out of it. I love this damn army coat, I really do.

"What part of the city are you from?"

I pause. My mind races with all of the possible answers I could give. Maybe I am too tired to say anything but the truth. "I'm from just outside the city actually. Small town."

"Okay. What are you doing here?"

"I don't know. I needed to get away for a while."

"You have a family there."

"Not really. I mean, I do, but not like a real one. It's just my dad and me and we don't get along very well."

"So you're just walking around drunk, looking for

Faran Bird?" She is staring at me funny and I wish it was earlier in the evening so I can see her face better. I can't tell what she is thinking.

"I guess so. I mean, it isn't supposed to be like this but that's how it ended up. You can't always plan how things are going to end up, you know."

We cross over Idylwyld and start heading up Twentieth Street. Except for a few cars in the distance, we are alone.

"I haven't been down here since I was a kid," I keep looking in all the windows of the stores we pass. I'm a window shopper. That's what my mom used to say to me when she'd take me shopping downtown after we had gone to the library or something. We were window shopping. We would walk up and down Second Avenue for what seemed liked hours. We never really went *in* to any stores and we didn't stand outside any stores either, because you can't do that. You can't just stand outside of places. People don't like it. You have to go in or out and if neither, you have to keep moving. So we'd keep moving all damn day. I don't know why we just window shopped because I'm sure there was *some* store she wanted to go in to. Maybe it felt safer for her on the outside, I don't know. She was an odd duck.

"It's not too far now," Janice said.

"Okay."

"You can sit and drink your bottle and if you need a place to crash, it's no big deal."

"Okay."

We continue walking and I continue drinking. I don't *feel* like I am all that drunk but I must be. I keep bumping up against the sides of the stores we pass and then, when I try to correct myself, I stumble over to the far side of the sidewalk and almost walk out into the bloody street.

Lucky there is no traffic at this time of night, whatever time it is. I would have been 'just another drunk' stumbling down Twentieth if I got hit by a car. Never mind anything else about me.

Finally Janice has had enough. She walks over and grabs my arm. She pulls me close so I can use her as a guide as we walk. It is like we are bloody boyfriend and girlfriend or something. We are coming home from the high school dance. One of the other boys spiked the punch bowl, I think. I don't know for *sure* though because I don't drink. I play hockey and I study hard in school because that's all I know how to do. That's what I will *always* do. My mom and dad are going to kill me when I get home. That is when Janice, my girlfriend, finally gets me home.

"Sorry," I said. "I can walk on my own, honestly. I wasn't paying attention, that's all."

"It's just easier this way." I know exactly what she means.

At first glance I think they are track marks.

Janice is standing under the lights from the sign of some Chinese restaurant. The lights shine on her arms and I see her try to cover them by turning away from me. Tiny zigzags on the underside of her forearm. We started walking again and as we approach the next street light I look back down at her arms. They aren't track marks. They are scars. Dark and purple. They look like they have been done a long time ago. Not too long ago, but long enough.

"What?" Janice is watching me watching her.

"I was just looking at your arms."

"Yeah," Janice laughs softly because it's easier. "I used to cut."

"That's okay."

Janice smiles. "I was going through some stuff and got too emotional. All girls get too emotional."

She is right about that. At school, you could always find a few girls with some scratches down their arms. Mostly the goth chicks but sometimes the regular magpies as well. These girls always made sure to wear t-shirts the next day so every damn person in the whole school knew they were feeling 'down' lately. They were just light scratches. One would have to pretty much saw off their arm to die from it. I should have brought a gun to school and said, "Here, you're doing it wrong. Use this." Then you could tell who was serious about it and you could get them some help before it was too late. Janice's scars aren't like the tiny cries for attention that ran up the arms of the girls in my school. Janice's scars are different. Deeper. Angry. Like she had put the knife in and twisted it around about a thousand times until all she could feel was the knife and her wounds, and finally, her scars. The same on the outside as they are on the inside. Not all scars are worn proudly, you know.

We don't say anything to each other for a while. Together, we walk along in the silence. I look up and try to see as far down twentieth as I can. The street dips and swerves and breaks off into two. I close one eye and try again but there is no change.

"I don't cut myself anymore," Janice said.

"I know." I don't know but it feels better to say that I do.

"I used to do it when I was high. I wouldn't even remember doing it until later. I'd wake up to pools of blood in my bed and on my clothes."

I don't want to hear anymore. I stop and take a few steps away from her. I twist the cap off of the vodka bottle and take a bigger sip than I want to. It takes all of my effort to choke it down. I feel my stomach burn and then lurch again.

"Are you okay?"

I drop to one knee and carefully place the bottle down on the sidewalk.

"Are you going to throw up?" Janice asks. She is beside me, her hand resting on my back.

I wave my hand at her, trying to brush her away but she stays. I close my eyes and try to concentrate on my breathing.

What are you doing out here you have to keep moving

"I know."

I swallow again and breathe. I will be all right for a little while.

"We're almost there."

I ask what time it is but it comes out broken and jagged.

She is beside me, her frail body holding my frail body up. As silent as ghosts, we haunt our way down twentieth.

TWENTY-ONE

We eventually find ourselves on Eighteenth Street. I feel like hours have passed. I close my eyes and just walk, trusting Janice to guide me.

Behind us, I hear something. The light scraping of feet against the cold pavement. Something clicks and clacks in steady rhythm and I *know* this sound. "Who's there?" I shout over my shoulder.

"Stop yelling," Janice squeezes my hand. "There's no one here but us."

But she's wrong. I stop and look behind us. In the far distance I see them. They slump and slouch towards us but they are so far away that I'm sure it will take all night for them to reach us. Yet, they are not so far away that I can't hear them. Their whispers carry in the air and when they reach me they quickly burrow into my head to keep warm.

"What are you looking at?" Janice looks into the distance but she doesn't see them. They are quick and ready. They hide in the shadows when she searches.

"My mom and my brother."

Janice looks again and I wonder why she cares so much to see. "What are you talking about? I don't see anyone."

You can't stand outside of places you have to go in or you
have to keep moving you can't

"Never mind them."

Janice shakes her head and turns. We continue walking
and as we do I hear the clicking again. It is faint but it is
there.

It is getting cold outside. I don't *feel* cold or anything
but every once in a while the wind would blow off of
the river and the chill of it would move into me. I should
have given Janice the coat a long time ago. She is probably
freezing to death out here.

"What are you doing?" Janice asks as I start taking the
coat off.

"I'm giving you the coat again. I'm too hot." I am pretty
drunk, I guess, because I am having a hell of a time pulling
the damn jacket off. It was like it was a part of me that I
had to hack off with a knife or something. My own shell.

"Are you sure? You look like you're still in rough shape.
You probably need it more than I do."

I really was too hot. There was a slick layer of sweat
on my forehead and body and the cool breeze feels nice
against my skin. "It's okay. Take it. I'll be fine."

I watch as she slowly pulls on the big coat. It's like
she is a little kid playing dress-up or something. This
is exactly what it looks like. Like she is running around
playing with her sister, her little sister, and they both got
into a big box of dad's old clothes. They think it will
be just about the funniest thing in the world to try on
one of dad's coats and take a walk around the block or
something. It is hard to imagine her as a kid which is
strange because I *always* imagine everyone as a kid. I can't
see it in her like I can in most people. When she wears my
army coat though, it's easier. I could imagine a whole new

life for her. She could be eight or nine or whatever her best years were.

"What kind of games did you play when you were young?" I ask. I am suddenly really curious about it but I also want her to talk so I can concentrate on her voice and not anything else.

She rolls up the sleeves of the coat as best as she can before she looks over at me and says, "What kind of games did I play? I don't know. I don't really remember."

"What do you mean you don't remember?" That kind of answer usually makes me mad. Most of the time, I don't even want to talk to someone anymore if they say they can't remember something as important as that. I'm not mad at her, I'm just frustrated. Everyone played *something* as a kid. How could you go and forget something like that. All the pure and nice things are there but we pile trash on top of them. We don't take the time to sift through. We forget about them and it's like they never happened.

"Don't get mad at me."

"No, I'm not mad," I said. I look at her so she can see that I'm serious. "I'm not mad. I just want you to remember."

"I didn't have a very good childhood. Maybe I don't want to remember it."

I think of my mom and my dad.

My brother.

One summer night when I was about seven we had had a barbeque in the backyard. Usually, mom made us go to bed early. She said that if we stayed up too late, it would 'ruin our brains'. Anyway, she must have let us 'ruin our brains' a little that night because we stayed out there until it was pitch black out. As a family. One of the only times I think we ever were. We sat on the back porch and had a hell of a time, laughing and joking around. Mom was telling us stories about the stars. They weren't crazy stories either because she wasn't all the way there yet. They were just normal stories, myths and Indian legends, things like that. My brother, being the clown that he is, was giving all the stars crazy names. Names like the 'Fart Star' and 'Swear Star' where all the aliens that lived there only spoke in swears. It was all pretty hilarious stuff for a seven-year-old to hear. My dad sat in his lawn chair, a little glass of whiskey in his hand, and quietly observed. Every once in a while, a deep chuckle would escape him and I remember laughing extra hard because it *must* have been funny when even my dad laughed. That night might have been the best night of my life. I think about it all the time and sometimes I even try to recreate it. I go outside and sit in the backyard. I look up at the sky and try to remember the stars my brother named. I hope my dad will come out and sit with me and we can talk. He doesn't, of course, but I still wish for it. I go back in the house and my brother's room is empty. My mom is gone too. My dad, passed out on the couch in his work clothes, a glass of whiskey on the floor beside him.

"Well, whatever," Janice replies as she keeps moving "We're almost there."

I follow after her as quickly as I can manage which isn't very fast. I try to calculate how long it has been since I have taken that little run on the football field. It hasn't been *that* long. It was just this afternoon. Wasn't I able to move a lot faster back then?

"My Grandma lives there," she said, pointing towards a beat up old shack beside us. The little shack looked like somebody's old garden shed or something. Cracked gray shingles covered both the roof and the walls and I was sure they were holding the whole house together. If a guy were to pull a few of those shingles off the whole place would have fallen over. A white picket fence surrounded the place and I'm not sure if it was to keep people out or to keep the two-foot tall weeds in. I think I would like to live in a place like this. A place that everyone else would hate to live in. I will let the weeds grow until they are damn near six feet tall. I'll water them and really get them sprouting. All my neighbors would be so pissed because you're not supposed to do things like that. You're supposed to make your yard look like everyone else's. I look at the house number but it doesn't ring a bell with me. I make a little mental note of it in my mind anyway so I'll remember it. If I ever get around to getting some money I'll buy the place.

"Are you close with her?" I ask.

"No. Not really. You have any Grandparents?"

"No. Well, I do, but not really."

"What do you mean?"

"My old man's parents died before I was even born so I never knew them. Miserable bastards, from what I hear, so it doesn't bother me too much. Mom's dad died when I was real young. Maybe two or so. Grandma's still alive somewhere but I never see her. She's in a home, I think. Dementia, Alzheimer's, I don't know. Something's wrong upstairs is all I know. The curse of our family, I guess."

"You guys are all crazy?"

"Everyone is crazy." I twist the top off of the vodka bottle and take a small drink.

We walk a little while in the silence. I feel too tired to talk and Janice doesn't seem to mind. People always think you have to talk. No one is comfortable in the silence. People can't just be with someone and say nothing. They think they have to say *something* because if they don't then there must be something wrong. I think it's the other way around. There's always something wrong when someone talks too much. I wonder if Janice spends as much time alone as I do. People who spend most of their time alone don't mind the silence. We prefer it.

I just wish Janice felt like talking.

They still slouch somewhere behind us. Their whispers are getting louder but I don't turn around. I don't indulge them. I can ignore them a little while longer.

I try to focus on a car I see parked along the side of the street. The car is maybe twenty or thirty feet away from me and all I can see of it is the front end and the glint of the windshield glass.

"What kind of car is that?" I ask.

"What?"

"See that car up ahead?" I hold out my finger like a pistol. "What kind of car is that?" From where we are walking I swear it's a Mustang. Same color as my brother's car. I must be really fucking plastered because I start thinking that maybe it *was* my brother's car. It wasn't in the garage at home anymore. It's here. Parked on Eighteenth Street. Maybe he has seen enough and has finally come to pick me up. I will have to ride in the back because the note he left is riding shotgun and I'd rather not be anywhere near it.

"I'm not sure," Janice said. "I don't know anything about cars."

I stop walking so I can steady myself long enough to take a good look at the car. I want to see if there is someone in the driver's seat. I need to know if someone is driving.

"What are you doing?" Janice calls to me.

I call out my brother's name and the sound is strange in this air.

"Who are you calling?"

Then I see him. He is blue again and if I reach out his skin will be cold. I move towards him and just as I do he is gone once more. He was never there. The car is empty and always has been.

A sudden moment of clarity drops on me and I remember that Jason has taken the car. He must have dropped it off here. I run towards the car and now I am angry instead of confused. "Why would you leave it here? Why would you leave it way the hell out here?"

Janice flutters over towards me and grabs my arm. "What's going on? Who are you yelling at?"

I stop yelling for a second and look at her. She has her back to the streetlight and I can't see her face too well. It might have calmed me down a little if I could see her face instead of just the blackness. My heart pounds in my chest and I struggle to back away from her. She is so small but she holds me firm. I can't break away.

"You need to stop yelling," she said because she doesn't understand.

I look back over her shoulder at the car. It isn't a Mustang anymore. It's someone's old Trans-Am. It has always been an old Trans-Am. From this angle I can see that it is black with blue stripes and that it doesn't look anything like my brother's car. I think I left the Mustang near the University. "I'm sorry," I say as politely as I can stand it. "There's not enough lights out here. Why would they think people want to walk around in the damn dark all day? Why don't they put up some fucking lights?"

"I don't know," Janice says and I notice her voice is tired. She is getting irritated with me, I can tell. It's only because she doesn't understand. I thought she did but I was wrong. I exist in a world that makes clear and absolute sense only to me.

"I'm sorry," I mumble. I fumbled with the liquor bottle for a bit before I manage to get the top off.

"Listen to me," Janice says, placing her hand on the bottle. "Maybe you should lay off the booze until we get there. If you pass out in the street I won't be able to carry you."

"I'm not too bad," I say. But I am bad. I feel dizzy and nauseous and my body won't stop shaking. There is not a time left in my hour glass.

"It's only up the street a little."

"How far is it?" I ask.

Janice gently screws the cap back on my bottle. She starts back up the street, the bottle tucked carefully in the crook of her arm.

I catch up to her but it takes me a while because my stomach is killing me. I wonder if I am slowly dying from it. A shard of broken glass is slowly cutting up my insides and I am bleeding to death. Inside. The wounds don't have time to scar over because you can't even see them. I will just get worse and worse and then that will be it. I suppose it is better going this way than a lot of other ways you could go. I'll have time to think a bit and realize I'm getting worse. Maybe tell people some secrets or something. It will be a whole lot better dying from this than by dying when you think everything is fine. When John Lennon was shot he was coming home from dinner. His last thoughts before that happened were probably about what he was going to watch on TV that night. There's no time to plan anything out with all the crazy ways a guy could go nowadays.

I twist my body a little so I can really get the blood flowing.

"It's that house on the end of the block there," Janice said, pointing down the street at a blur of dark shapes in the distance.

I nod, as if I can see what she is pointing at, but I can barely see my shoes straight.

"Yeah, you can crash in one of the bedrooms."

"Okay."

It takes all my strength just to count her footsteps as she moves through the darkness while the clicking of long dead high heels keeps an ever steady rhythm on the pavement behind us.

TWENTY-TWO

The deep bass of some muddled hip-hop song pounds in the nighttime air. It isn't until I am on the gravel driveway leading up to an older house that I realize that this is our destination and that this is where the music is coming from.

"Sounds like people are still up." Janice said.

I can hear the music more clearly as we walk up the cracked cement staircase towards the front door. The cement is cracked in such a way that you are forced to choose a side as you cross over it. You have to choose a side every time you walk here and I wonder if it drives the people who live here crazy.

A screen door hangs on rusted hinges and it creaks as Janice pulls it open. She pounds on the front door and we wait for several seconds. Then, realizing that no one is coming to let us in, she grabs hold of the door handle and twists. The door pops open with a rough thud and the strong smell of weed floats out.

Janice walks in and I follow but I am really uncomfortable doing it. I hate just walking into places. I need time to adjust. I need time to sit outside a while and get comfortable. Have a smoke or drink or something and then just sort of gradually blend in. I can't just be outside one second and all the way in the next.

The inside of the house looks exactly like I think it will look. A pair of beat up old couches in front of an old coffee table. On the dingy wall hangs a picture of Bob Marley smoking a joint because people who live in places like this think a picture like that is cool. The carpet is thin and grey or blue, I can't really tell because the light isn't all that bright in here. The whole place smells like dust, stale booze, and pot.

From the hallway, I see someone come out of one of the bedrooms. He is a bigger guy dressed in baggy dark jeans and a red t-shirt. Native. Tattoos run up both of his arms but they are too busy so I can't make out what they are. He carefully looks at me as we come into the living room. I wonder if this is Faran. For some reason, I don't think so.

"Hey," Janice said.

She turns to me and says, "This is Charlie."

"Who's this?" Charlie quickly demands.

Janice tells him who I am and what I'm doing there. He brushes by her and goes into the kitchen.

"Did my sister come around?"

"No, I saw her yesterday though."

Charlie is hunched over the stove. Stuck in the elements of the stove are two butter knives, their ends burnt black. On the counter are tiny green balls of weed. I haven't seen anyone hot-knifing in a while and it takes me a second to realize what he is doing.

Behind us, another girl comes into the kitchen. Native again. She has a heavy build and is much taller than me. She has long black hair that falls down her back and as she moves across the kitchen, the light makes her hair shine and sparkle. I think about growing my hair out and dying it black.

"Hi." The new girl mutters.

"This is Heather," Janice said to me.

I nod at Heather and watch as she walks over to Charlie. Charlie expertly grabs the knives and presses them neatly into one of the tiny balls of weed. He holds the knives up and lets Heather inhale the thin stream of smoke that floats up from the blades. Then, he repeats the steps and inhales the smoke himself.

Heather watches me carefully. "Do you want some?" she says.

I shake my head slowly and Janice answers for me. "He's a little partied out."

Charlie and Heather laugh and I smile with them because that's what you're supposed to do.

Heather looks over at Janice. "You see your sister yet?"

"No."

"I think she might have gone up to P.A. then."

"Where did you hear that?"

Heather paused long enough to suck up a little more smoke before she said, "Jackie and Donna went up there with Hunter."

"When?"

"Yesterday afternoon."

I see Janice visibly relax a little after she hears this new news on her sister. She looks back at me and smiles like we are both relieved by this news. It means nothing to me. Nothing at all.

"What are you wearing?" Heather laughs and the sound is strange and halting to my ears.

"Yeah, it's his," Janice said, slowly letting my old army coat off slip off her shoulders. She hands me my bottle of vodka so that she could finish cutting the damn coat off of herself.

"It's my old army coat," I whisper, a stupid smile frozen on my numb face.

"What army is that?" Charlie said. "The Salvation Army?"

Everyone in the room laughs and I go on smiling like a jackass. It is all I can really do right now.

Janice carefully places my coat over the arm of a kitchen chair that sits against a worn out table. I look at the coat and yearn to have enough energy to walk towards it and put it on. I wasn't cold or anything but I need to hide in it for a while. To fall asleep with it draped over me so that I can smell the cigarette smoke and the stains and run my fingers over the patches. I start to walk towards it but the earth suddenly tilts and I almost fall to the dirty kitchen floor.

Janice grabs my arm again and helps me into the living room. The couch seems to race towards me and before I can brace for impact, I fall forward into the soft cushions. I feel my bottle fall out of my hand. It rolls to the edge of the couch by my feet but I don't have the energy to pick it up.

"Go to one of the rooms if you're going to pass out," Janice said, sitting down beside me. Charlie flops down on the other couch while Heather stands watch from the doorway.

"I'm fine," I said. "I'm not going to pass out. I'm going to die."

I laugh again because everyone else is laughing.

I hear something scraping against the door. The creaking of the screen and the rush of whispers just outside. "Come in," I shout.

You can't just come in to places

"There's no one out there," Charlie's gruff voice rings out.

Janice sees me fumbling with the bottle cap again and she says, "Hold on. I can't stand watching you drink out of that huge bottle anymore." She springs up from the couch and returns a few moments later with a can of beer in her hand. She carefully places the cold aluminum can into my shaking hands. She takes the unopened bottle of vodka and holds it in her lap.

"What are you doing here?" Charlie is looking at me with strange and vacant eyes. "I think you're in the wrong house."

"Leave him alone," Janice sighs.

"This is Indian land you're on, don't you know that, brother?" He is smiling as he speaks but I know there is something wrong.

"You can't be here if you're not one of us," he continues.

"I'm Métis," I manage to say.

Charlie says something to me but his accent is thickened by the weed and I can hardly make out what he is saying.

"What?"

"I said something to you in Cree."

I think this is his way of saying I am a stranger here. I am cut off so far that I can't even understand the language.

Charlie and Heather laugh.

I smile.

Janice shifts uncomfortably in her chair.

"What do you know about the Métis then," Heather joins in on the fun.

"I don't know," I say, after thinking about her question

for a thousand years or so. "I never really had anyone to teach me." I wish I knew *something* so I could talk about it a little. I don't know a damn thing about me or the Métis or anything. I feel like I should know.

"You know when the Métis got started?" Heather asks.

I swallow some beer before slowly shaking my head.

"About nine months after the white man landed on the shores." She laughs again and so does Charlie. There laughter is loud and real and I wish I could laugh along with them. I try to remember the last time I have laughed for real.

"You don't look like you got much Indian in you," Charlie said.

"My mom," I whisper.

"Your mom? Your mom had a few Indians in her?" Charlie laughs and this time I sense hatred towards me.

"Leave him alone," Janice says again. "He's had a rough night."

"Make him go lay down," Heather said.

Janice stands up in front of me. She helps to hoist me up so I can stand again. She turns her gaze back to Heather. "You see Faran around today?"

"I never saw him but Dakota is in the other room," Heather said.

"He'll probably stop by in a bit," Charlie cuts in.

I drain a little more of my beer and let Janice lead me out of the room and down the dark hallway.

"Don't sleep with her," Charlie growls.

Charlie's voice is deep and cold and I get the sense he wants to kill me. It's okay though. I understand. Really, I do.

Janice walks ahead of me down the small highway. She doesn't turn any lights on and I'm glad. I don't want to see any pictures of these people. I don't want to see them when they are young.

"We can sleep in here," Janice says as she opens the door to a small room at the end of the hallway. A single mattress lays pushed up against the far wall. There is no furniture of any kind and we have to walk over a pile of clothes to get to the bed. Beside the bed is a small alarm clock sitting on the floor. The numbers read 1:39.

"Who is Dakota?" I ask but I feel like I already know the answer.

"That's Faran's son. He stays here a lot because Heather takes care of him.

I think about her words for a moment. I picture a small boy in one of the other rooms. Right now he's dreaming about what he wants to be when he grows up. There is nothing bad in his world.

This doesn't change anything for me.

"Can you get my bottle?" I say carefully.

Janice looks at me for a second before she walks out of the room.

I bring my beer up to my mouth and empty the small can. I let it fall from my hands and onto the floor. I crawl into bed and lay my head down.

I lay in the dark and wait for Janice to return with my bottle. I will wait here until I hear Faran Bird come. Then, I will take my gun and I will shoot him. This is my plan.

Sleep comes too easily as I sit here waiting for Janice. I feel myself drifting off, my hand clutched around the handle of my gun and my mind filled with the whispers of my family.

TWENTY-THREE

I am torn from sleep.

Before I can even open my eyes, I feel waves of panic washing over me. My heart is pounding and my breath is caught somewhere between my throat and wherever it enters my lungs. I roll over and try to ground my chest into the mattress so I can't feel my heart beating so fast.

I am in a bedroom on Eighteenth.

The realization of where I am and how I got here comes fast and hard.

Hillary, Heather, I don't know.

Charlie.

Dakota.

No.

I look over and in the dim light of the room I see Janice curled up on a pile of clothes. Like a little kid who has fallen asleep playing or something. I want to wake her so I can find my bottle.

I hear laughter from the living room and the slight vibration of music lightly rattling the bedroom door. I wonder how many more people are out there. I wish I was a ghost again so I can see.

Yet, somehow I know. I *know.*

Faran Bird is in this house. He is home and in front of

him is all the tinsel and shiny things that he will use to decorate his nest. I won't miss this time.

Faran Bird has important work to do

I look down at the little alarm clock. 3:22. Behind the clock, illuminated just slightly by the red light of the numbers, I see my bottle. I rush towards it, my hands closing around the thin glass neck. I frantically fumble with the top and once it is opened, the sharp smell of alcohol rises up and chokes me, making my ribs shiver with nausea. Just one sip. I may need to be steady.

I sit on the edge of the mattress and concentrate on the sounds of my breathing. I am so tired and my body feels rigid and stiff. When this is over, when this is *all* over, I will sleep for so long.

Janice is in a deep sleep and before I leave this room I want to watch her for a while. I like to watch people as they sleep. You can imagine them as a kid and listen to the sounds of their breath and wonder about all the things they dream about. The secrets they never tell anyone.

When I was young, I used to sneak into my parent's room late at night and watch them sleep. Dad was a fairly good sleeper, didn't make too much noise or anything. Old mom though, she was crazy even when she slept. Talking and yelling and thrashing about while she carried on conversations with all the demons that haunted her. She never had any peace. Not even for one second. When she drowned herself I wonder if she was actually trying to drown those horrible demons.

I used to watch my brother sleep too. He always slept with his headphones on, blasting tunes. Always. The music was usually loud enough that I could make out the words from across the room. It made you wonder how a guy could sleep that way. I tried it a few times but it wasn't my thing. It made me think too much. My bro was a real peaceful sleeper, no snoring or moving about. I liked to watch him sleep most of all. I think it's because he was such a deep thinker and was always telling me these cool stories or ideas he had come up with. I imagined his dreams were filled with these stories and ideas and that a guy could get lost in them forever if he liked.

I didn't want to go to his funeral. I was scared of seeing his dead body. Everyone told me that 'it was just like he was sleeping' so I went. I wanted to watch him sleeping one last time. It wasn't like he was sleeping. Not at all. He was laying there and he looked waxy and different and his hair wasn't the way he would have liked. I started yelling that he needed his headphones and that when he slept. He liked his damn headphones on. Some bastard I had never even met before took me out of there while I was screaming about it. All I wanted to do was put his damn headphones on. People always think they know what's best for someone else.

Janice is such a soft breather I almost want to reach out and check for a pulse. I know she's just sleeping. She's somewhere else right now. She is playing all the games she played as a kid before time stole them away from her.

I lean down to pull her blanket up over her and realize it isn't a blanket but my old army coat. She has pulled it over her and because she is so small it was almost like a damn sleeping bag. I leave it on her. It feels right that she has it. I could have gently pulled it off her and covered her up with something else but I don't want to. I think that maybe she will need it more than I ever will again. It's an ugly old coat anyway, you know.

Go shoot him

The sound is cold and metallic in my ear. It startles me and I feel my breath quicken. "Isn't there another way?"

He is a magpie a magpie a magpie a magpie

Then suddenly, I hear my mom's voice. Yet, this is not how she sounded when I knew her. This is her new voice now. It's like whispering rushing water that bends and stretches over the ridges and valleys of my mind. You can hardly ever make out what she's saying. Just that terrible rushing whisper.

Your brother is broken all over the floor

What's he doing what's he doing what's he doing

"I don't know. Just let me think for one second." I try to keep quiet. I don't want to wake poor Janice.

He sits so carefully on the fence with all of his drugs

"I never tried to actually shoot the magpie that day. I made sure the pellet gun's barrel was slightly to the left. He *knew* that too. He didn't even flinch. He stayed on the fence and his feathers were so quiet and still."

You missed the magpie and you killed the robin

"I didn't mean to."

The magpie killed the robin because you didn't kill the magpie

I stand on my tired and sore legs and move towards the bedroom door.

I open the door just slightly and listen.

There is more laughter. Charlie and a few other male voices. The strong smell of marijuana and smoke, and something acrid.

I creep out into the hallway and quietly close the door. The thought of saying goodbye to Janice crosses my mind but I think she would prefer it this way.

The hallway is dark and is my last refuge. I can't stay here forever and I will have to keep moving.

I tuck the bottle of vodka into the waist band of my jeans. It is uncomfortable but I think I'd like to take it with me and I need my hands free.

I am half-way down the hall when Charlie passes by from the kitchen on his way to the living room. He stares at me with eyes that are huge and wild. I know at once that he is high on something a lot stronger than weed.

"Hey," he slurs, taking a step forward. "Did you mess around with her?"

I smile because I am nervous and scared and don't know what else to do. "No, I fell asleep."

Charlie laughs and the sound is strange and foreign. The drugs and drink have twisted up his vocal cords. He scratches at his face and walks down the hallway towards me.

"C'mon buddy," he said, grabbing me by my arm. "Come sit with us in the living room."

I let him pull me along because I don't know what else to do.

We enter the living room and I see immediately what he has been up to in the few hours I have slept.

On the beat-up old couch, two other Native guys sit stiffly. One is dressed in red. He wears tinted sunglasses even though the room is dark. The other is in a white coat with a fake fur collar and his eyes are as crazy and as empty as Charlie's. On a chair near the front door, I see Shay. He is smiling at me while his hands pick at a scab that had formed over the cuts on his face. On the coffee table I see tinfoil. A broken light bulb. The jagged pieces of glass singed black. Meth crystals laid out so carefully and cautiously. A few beer cans and a mickey of whiskey sit patiently on the floor. A rap song quietly leaks from the stereo speakers.

"Sit down, brother." Charlie said.

I sit on the floor beside the couch and wonder who of these lost people is Faran Bird. I don't think any of them are.

After the day I shot the robin, I became obsessed with getting the magpie on the fence. It wasn't *right* that he escaped. Every time I went out with a pellet gun or slingshot, I could never find one of the ugly bastards. I'd turn down an alley and they'd fly away. They're cunning. They *sense* danger. As soon as I didn't have a gun on me, I'd see hundreds of them. They would watch me with their black eyes as I walked right by them. They know I am not a threat.

"Have a drink," Charlie slurs again.

I reach over and take a beer. I'm content just to hold it in my hands and it remains unopened.

No one introduces themselves but I think it is too late for that. I am in the presence of ghosts now and ghosts no longer have names. Every one of them is off in their own world, haunting what they can find. Charlie looks at me again while he haunts but I can't be sure whether he sees me or not.

The guy in the white coat with the fake fur collar is talking to himself. Quick little mutterings while grinding his teeth. In one of his hands he holds a piece of glass from the broken light bulb. A small grey chunk of crystal meth balancing on the smooth surface. He holds the plate of glass up to his mouth and Charlie leans forward with his lighter. He lets the small flame heat up the glass and the meth until a thin blue line of smoke snakes up from the heat. Fur Collar unclenches his jaw just long enough to suck up the smoke.

"You were fucking Janice." Charlie curls his hand out

towards me and slowly closes his fist. I wasn't sure whether he is threatening me or if it's something the meth makes him do.

"No, honestly I wasn't." I grip the beer so tightly.

"What are you doing here?" The guy in the red shirt and shades looks at me. He seems to be more alert than the others. He pulls off his sunglasses and stares with bloodshot eyes that are as crazy as Charlie's and Fur Collar's but much more present.

A demon.

"I don't know."

Charlie and Sunglasses laugh.

"Are you looking for something?" Sunglasses asks, leaning forward.

"I don't know," I say again.

"You don't know?"

"No, I don't know. I wish I did but I don't."

Words from Sunglasses I can't understand. I realize he is speaking Cree. They flow out of his mouth perfect and smooth like a song.

Shay stops scratching long enough to look up at Sunglasses. He speaks in the same smooth and perfect pitch of their shared language. Sunglasses replies and they stare at each other in the silence afterward.

I realize I am not a ghost.

"Don't you speak our language?" Sunglasses asks.

"No."

Sunglasses laughs at me before pulling his shades back down. He sinks back into the worn cushions of the couch.

"Here, you smoke this," Charlie said, dropping some meth onto the burnt shard of glass. "Then you can speak in any language."

I looked at the tiny sliver of drug and say, "No, I can't. I don't smoke meth."

"Yes, you do," Sunglasses said, standing up from the couch. He grabs the mickey of whiskey and takes a quick slug of it before letting the plastic bottle drop to the floor. He reaches into the waistband of his jeans and pulls out a small gun that looks identical to the once Shay had shown me earlier. He places it down on the coffee table.

"What's your name?" I blurt out suddenly.

Sunglasses looks over at Shay and smiles like he can't believe I would ask such a thing.

"That's not who you were looking for earlier," Shay said. He makes eye contact with me and I believe him.

Sunglasses stands over me. I can't bring myself to look up at him and meet his eyes.

"Smoke it," he demands.

"I can't," I say again.

"Smoke it."

"Please," I whisper.

Charlie says something that I can't understand. He reaches over and slaps me across the face and the sound is clear and crisp in my ear. I don't feel it all. It exists somewhere outside of me.

"You better smoke some," Shay said from across the room. "He'll kill you."

Sunglasses turns and says something to Shay. Shay laughs and so does Fur Collar.

"I can't," I say again. "I have important work to do." Now I am crying. I can feel tears rolling down my face and into the corners of my mouth. I taste the salt and the dirt and the blood and I swallow. I swallow again and feel my stomach twist and heave.

My head is jerked back violently as Charlie, or someone

else, tugs hard on my hair. I look up because for some reason I want to see who has pulled. All I can make out through my tears is a blur of colors and shapes.

Charlie presses the broken light bulb up to my face. I hear the click of the lighter. The click of the lighter again. I think that maybe it is out of fluid and I open my eyes to see. The flame leaps up and spreads over the black glass. I close my eyes and try to turn my head away from the blue smoke but I can't. Their hands hold me still.

"You better smoke it," my brother calls from across the room.

I open my eyes again and see him watching me. He is re-stringing my guitar in the corner and smiling at me. His ear phones are in and I think it is because he doesn't care much for rap either.

I look down and see the dirty grey crystal smoking and burning. A thin line of smoke. I smell it and for some reason I think of the elementary school and the floor cleaner. All the perfect little muddy foot prints being mopped away forever.

I let the smoke in and feel my heart hammer in my chest.

They are laughing. Some more words that I can't understand. Then I am falling and I smell the cigarette smoke and the dirt of the worn carpet of the living room. I push myself up and crawl along the floor while my stomach heaves.

Blood and water and a sick yellow stream pour from my mouth and onto the floor in front of me. I fall into it and it coats my face and neck. My fingers grasp the edge of the coffee table. From the corner of my vision, I see the amber whiskey bottle. My hand flicks out faster than it should have. Faster than it could have. I can't reach the bottle and I question if it really even there. Just another ghost.

I have to keep moving.

I puked again. Violent and yellow. I let myself fall back to the carpet and for a brief moment I think that nothing else could ever be as comfortable. Then it is gone and I am suddenly swallowing whiskey from the plastic bottle.

Strong arms pull me up and I feel as though I am standing on legs that aren't mine. Charlie looks at me and I try to see past his eyes. He opens his mouth and tries to speak but smoke rolls out instead. He blows it into my face and I think I understand what he is doing. I think it is a gift and he hopes I will understand.

I open my mouth to speak but nothing comes out because I am empty.

Shards of reality cut into my mind. I swallow again. Then the bottle is taken from my hand. My brother, maybe. I don't know. I whirl about the room looking for him so I can ask him where he has found the strings. But I already know. He never has to search around for strings, like me, because he always has them. He will never run out of strings.

He is in front of me. I reach out and grab hold of him and bring his face to mine. The world goes silent and quiet and together we exist somewhere outside of this space.

"Hey," he says. "He's outside."

He let's go of my arms and in the next moment he is gone. I am thrust back into this living room on Eighteenth.

I see the front door but it is too far away to walk. Suddenly, I am there and I feel the grooves and hardness against my hand. I grip the round handle and pull while the outside air rushes forward to embrace me.

Someone speaks to me but I can't understand. I nod in the general direction of the shapes because a guy has to do *something* when he's leaving. Quickly and quietly, I walk out of the house and into the blackness of the night.

TWENTY-FOUR

I should have known it would still be dark out but for some reason it came as a shock. Usually, I like it when it's dark. Like at home, when I go for my walks and there's no one out and I can go to all the places in town that I like to go. I can see how all of the places have changed because I can inspect them really close. During the day someone would be watching me, but not at night. I'm free to haunt where I want.

This is different. I am scared of this dark. I am afraid of getting lost. Dying in the street and no one finding me because it is too dark. They would think it was drugs and I can't handle that.

I stumble over the lawn of the small house where inside Janice sleeps and the ghosts are smoking meth. I figure I should get away from this place as soon as possible. Any place would be better.

Then I see him. He is leaning against the hood of a car, smoking a cigarette. He is doing something with his cell phone but he puts it away in his pocket as I approach.

"I hear you were looking for me."

His voice is high pitched, almost feminine. He is thin and his hair is long, almost like mine. He wears a dark jacket and a blood red sweater. It is too dark to see his face clearly so I move closer. "You're Faran?"

"Yes. What do you want?"

I wonder if this is the same question he asked my brother and I have to think about his answer for a while.

"I think you knew my brother."

The world seems so impossibly clear right now in this darkness. There's vividness to the colors and even though everything is moving too fast, it all makes perfect sense.

"I might. I know a lot of people."

I watch his movements. They are so careful and deliberate. His hand with the cigarette moves from his side to his mouth in one fluid motion. He is like a clock.

"What are you doing here?" I ask.

"My son is here," he said, motioning with his free hand towards the house. "He's asleep in the house."

"What does he want to be when he grows up?" I ask because I have to know. I *have* to before it's all too late and there's still time.

Faran Bird takes a drag on his cigarette and looks over at me. In this light I can't guess his age. It's impossible to tell. He is so much smaller and frail than the monster from my dreams.

He looks so much like me.

"He wants to be a cop," a small smile forms on his face. "Imagine that."

I nod, and as I do I feel for the gun in my waistband. It is there waiting politely beside my bottle of liquor. I reach down and pull the liquor out first.

"Do you want a drink?" I ask.

He looks at the bottle and then shakes his head. For a brief moment I think I get a clear look at his intentions. He has to do *something* out here, after all. He's just sitting there. It's me that came to him. It's me that doesn't have a reason.

"So, what do you want?" He asks again.

I slowly twist off the top of the bottle and take one long sip. It will be enough so I calmly slip it back into the waistband of my jeans. I notice Faran watching me from his shadow.

"Are you going to shoot me?" His words are so calm that they cause my skin to prickle and bump.

"What?"

He takes another drag on his cigarette and looks back over at me. "You have a gun in your waistband and I'm asking if you're here to shoot me."

I reach down and calmly pull the gun out. It feels so heavy in my hands and I wonder how someone in the army could lug around a machine gun all day.

"I have to," I whisper. "You *know* that, right?"

Faran Bird lets his black jacket fall off of his frail shoulders. It lies still on the car hood and I wonder why he took it off. He pulls at the sleeve of his red sweater as if it suddenly feels strange and foreign against his skin. He leans his head back and I watch as a thin tendril of smoke slowly rises from his mouth. "It wasn't me who killed him. You *know* that, right?"

He's so calm that I can't stand it. A part of me wants him to be scared, pleading with me to save his life. I wonder if he has accepted death and is more than willing to take a bullet and end it all.

It hits me with simple clarity. He is not scared because he doesn't think I will do it. He sees no threat and a magpie won't fly away if there isn't a threat. They stay and taunt. It is part of their prize.

He turns and looks at me and his eyes are beady and

black. I watch as the cool early morning air rustles his feathers. He sits and waits so patiently and it is enough to drive me mad.

I raise the gun slowly and as I do, I see something in his face change. He has made a mistake and he is surprised in the simple clarity of it all as well. "Wait," he manages to say as he slides off the car hood and faces me. He is still and silent as he watches.

His body tenses and he is about to move when I pull the trigger. The bullet catches him somewhere in his beautiful red chest and he crumples to the ground, as still and silent in death as he was in his last moments of life.

I put the gun back in my waistband, thankful it is no longer in my hands. Then, as silent as a ghost, I disappear further into the darkness ahead.

TWENTY-FIVE

It's a funny place down here in the Alphabet Jungle. That's what they call it. The Alphabet Jungle. All the Avenues from D to W. I guess they call it a jungle because of all that happens in these streets. It's dangerous, just like a real jungle, and you have to know where to walk. You'll end up dead. Stuck in the ribs by a morphine addict. Swallowed by a snake. In the end, there is little difference. Creatures just doing what they do.

I stumble down these streets and while I move I think about how the trees seem darker than they should be. Darker than they could be. I look up at them and for a moment I believe they have pushed their way in through rips in the sky. Like the sky has been torn and slashed and the great flaps of cut sky were hanging loose and the black shape of the trees is what it looked like on the other side. Nothing. Black and empty.

I try to see anything up the road. Anything at all to put some distance between myself and all that is behind me.

I place my hand on the cool bottle that is against my stomach. I felt the weight and texture of it and I know it is real. I pull the bottle out of my pants and hold it up to eye level. A bit left. Hopefully enough to get me home.

Home.

I look forward to the moment when I can finally go home for good. The old man will probably be dead by then, which will be no big deal, but even if he is alive I have no problem pouring him drinks and looking for his lighter until he goes. I'll probably need the rituals to keep me sane by that point anyway. We're all one step away from the loony bin without our rituals, you know. I'll close up the windows and exist in my world and be perfectly happy. Alone. I suppose I might need *some* money so I'll probably put out a *'Best Of' album* every once in a while. The Best of me.

You killed him

There is no one out here so I walk down the middle of the street. I'm not even sure what street it is. It feels safer out here instead of on the sidewalk. I am as far away from the blackness as possible.

It smells like rain but I don't think it's rained since yesterday afternoon. When I was on the football field. I remember the rain and how it felt as it fell against my face. I'm sure it existed in a place outside my mind but now I'm not so sure.

Tiny sounds hiss and crackle in the air around me. Simple messages that float within the radio waves. I'm scared of the darkness and I wonder if I'll be able to hide in these sounds for a while.

There is a pair of cars parked along the street up ahead. I think I see someone sitting in the front seat. The person is talking to someone in the passenger seat who is crouched down and hiding. I can hear their hurried voices but not clear enough to make out what they are saying.

I walk towards the car slowly but I stop when I am ten-feet away. As soon as I am still the voices grow quiet.

It is my brother's car. This time, I am sure of it.

I see the curve of the body over the rear wheel and I remember the first time I ran my hand over this spot. There is the racing stripe, as I remember it. A thin strip running the length of the car separating it down the middle. I wonder how the car can be here and for a quick jangled second I think my brother has come to pick me up.

He rolls down the window and it takes a while because you have to do it by hand.

"What are you doing here?" I ask. I stay in the shadows and make no effort to move closer.

"I came to pick you up. You're done now. All your important work is done and you can rest." He keeps his eyes on the road ahead of us. One hand rests casually on the steering wheel, just like it always has. He's so still. I want to move closer just so I can see him move, but I can't.

"Are you coming?"

"I can't," I whisper. 'I mean, I don't want to."

"Why? Mom's not here, you know." His voice is flat and emotionless and there's a weariness to it like it's been a long night.

"You killed him."

"Yeah. I mean, I don't know. I think so. I shot him in the chest." I scratch at my head as I speak because suddenly it is so damn itchy.

"You have to leave this place now. That's what you wanted."

I start walking up the street so I can think things through for a second. I can't be looking at him and that car and make any sort of rational decision. What I need to do is just put a little space between me and all that is behind.

"Where are you going?" I hear him call out.

"I...I don't know. I'll meet you later." I look straight ahead and keep walking and in the distance I can see a thin shade of light rising. "Just leave me alone, for a bit."

"You made a choice. You chose a side and went in. You can't go back out now."

"I know."

"He had a child."

"I...don't know."

I'm going to lose it if I'm not careful. I can feel little bits of my mind slowly falling through and when you get to that point, you can't save them all. Bits will still get through and if you let go to try to save those bits then the rest will come crashing after it. I just need to stay calm and think. That's all a guy needs sometime, you know.

When my mom was near the end, and the edges were really caving in on her, she still tried to keep things normal. They weren't normal, and I think she knew that, but they were normal enough for a young child who hardly knew the difference. I remember coming home from school one day and finding the kitchen in a hell of a mess. Flour and sugar spilled all over the damn place and pots and pans on the floor. Every cupboard was open and the microwave running and set for forty minutes with nothing inside of it. My mom was in her usual day wear of panties and high-heels. She had made me a sandwich. Two pieces of white bread covered in a blanket of ketchup. In the middle of the ketchup there was nine multi-vitamins arranged into the shape of a cross. She told me it was healthy for me and that the sandwich would cleanse me inside and out. I ate it because she wanted me too and all good boys do what their mothers want them to do. While I ate, she told me about all the people that were living inside of one of our neighbors and how she had figured out this fun little fact by assigning numbers to the letters in the books she had brought home from the library.

Our poor mother.

I just have to keep moving and as I do, I think of the fire alarm I pulled back at my old school. The thought of it just drops into my mind and I wonder what brought it here because up until this moment, the fire alarm never bothered me at all.

You are a murderer

I pulled the fire alarm because I am a magpie who only thinks of himself. At the time I thought the kids would find it funny. I probably scared them. I was always scared of the fire alarm as a kid. It was sharper and louder than the recess bell and it always made us jump anytime it went off.

I should have left it alone. I should have left everybody alone.

I listen to the sound of my feet as I walk over the cold pavement. It has probably been a hundred years or so since these streets were gravel roads. I wonder if there is anyone still alive who remembers what it sounded like when you walked over the gravel in this area.

A car passes me on my left and it scares the shit out of me because I don't hear it coming. The car looks like my brother's again. I see the racing stripe running up the back of it. He must be trying to catch up to me. He wants to know if I have changed my mind. My time is almost up and he has to find me before it was too late. Too late for what? I don't know. Until they pour pavement over me, I guess, and no one remembers one damn thing about me. I bet he can't concentrate on finding me because Mom is in the passenger seat and is probably talking his ear off. Telling him all about some new secrets she found down at the library. It will be good to see her again. I will sit down with her and make her tell me a story. It won't scare me this time.

I know better now.

Up ahead the car turns left and I see that it isn't the Mustang. It is an old Crown Vic. Not even close. I guess the early morning light must have been playing with my eyes or something. Cancel the family reunion for just a little while longer.

It is getting brighter all the time and I am thinking it is going to be a hell of a nice day. Maybe, if I felt okay, I'll forget about going home and head down to the river or something. Relax along the riverbank while I imagine how far my mom's body travelled before they fished her out. They don't tell you those details when you're a kid. Things like how far your mom's body travelled down the river after she jumped into it and drowned. 'Your mom drowned in the river' is pretty much the extent of it. 'A suicide', they say and you're left pondering over that word for the next ten years wishing they had just said everything at once.

I sort of feel myself going right about now. Like my heart is skipping a beat every now and then. Beating on the other side. Everything flickers and goes black just for a second before snapping back into focus. I am too tired to be scared anymore.

I keep walking. It is all I can really do.

I think I see him before he sees me but they're tricksters, those birds. The magpie is perched on a street sign. He cries out once and the sound is jarring and terrible. The rest of the world has gone and died and all I am left with is this ugly, vain, bird and his terrible cry.

"You're dead," I yell at him.

He turns and looks at me and I swear he smiles.

Then, I feel the bottle of vodka in my hand. It is real and when I lift it to eye level I hear the liquor inside as it ebbs and flows.

I move to the side of the street and sit on someone's grass made wet by the early morning dew. It is here where I slowly twist the cap off and tilt the bottle to my lips. I swallow more than I need to but everything is okay.

I fall against the grass and feel the cold wetness starting to coat my jeans and the bottom of my t-shirt and my hands.

My heart jumps as I hear the awful cries of the magpie directly behind me. I turn and see him perched on the tiny picket fence of the neighboring house. He is watching me. No, he is watching something else. He has his beady eyes on the cap of my vodka bottle. The bright red top that stands out like a diamond in this bleak and colorless world.

His envy is part of my prize.

I take the cap off and lift the bottle to my mouth once more. My face is pressed into the grass and I think about never moving again. I clutch the bottle cap tightly in my hand so the damn bird can't even see it.

I open my eyes. The magpie still watches.

The bottle has a few good swallows in it. Slowly, and with great effort, I pull myself up. I stand there as still as I can stand it. Another quick drink followed by another. My stomach seizes up. Vomit. Harsh and tearing and I fall back to the grass, my face and chest against the bloody and yellow mess that has just escaped me. I feel myself drifting off but I fight it hard. Not yet. Not until I am done. Then I can go.

I open my eyes and see that he has moved. He is on the grass now. Only a few feet away from me. Watching.

"Your life is useless," I manage. "Running around collecting your dirty little trinkets to impress all of your friends."

He cocks his head as if this is some great realization to him.

I pull the bottle to my lips and do my best to pour into my mouth. Most of it rolls down my cheek but I get some of it.

My hand opens and I see the bright red cap. I let it fall from my fingers and it rolls a few inches from my outstretched hand.

"Take it."

He looks at me like I am the trickster. He hops a few inches closer. His movements are fast and unpredictable and I close my eyes to escape them. When I open them again I see the cap clutched carefully in his beak. He looks at me. His eyes are full of pride and vanity and accomplishment. He has an audience and there really isn't a point if one doesn't have an audience. This is all that matters to the magpies of the world and to those like them. All of the bright and shiny objects.

He continues to watch me. He has his prize but he doesn't fly away.

I feel a wave of anger wash over me. My hand gropes for the gun in my waistband. I feel my fingers grip the cold metal handle and the weight of it is comforting. In an instant the gun is out and I level it at his head. I am shaking but I don't think it will matter. I can't miss from this close. I will never miss another magpie again.

The magpie makes no attempt to escape. He sits there, his head twitching from side to side while he holds my red bottle cap in his beak.

"Go on," I shout. "Do you want to die? Do you think I won't shoot you?"

I feel my finger curl around the trigger and just as I am about to pull, the magpie flaps his wings once and flies away.

Anguish seeps from me and I cry out in pain. I think suddenly of the war with the Grade Sixes and Luke Rocket's hands. I think of the recess bell and how I forgot how the damn place smelled.

Shay and Janice. My coat protecting her for a little while but soon it wouldn't be enough. I knew that. We both *knew* that.

Above me, I see the magpie flying away, the red bottle cap bright against the gray above. Then in this moment I know it doesn't matter that I missed him because I could never get them all. I could never get rid of all the magpies.

I lift the gun up and press the barrel hard against my skull. I feel my finger tighten around the trigger and this time I pull.

The morning air is not ripped apart by the blast from the pistol. It remains peaceful and silent except for a light breeze that rustles the leaves of a tree somewhere to my left.

I open my eyes and I see that my hand is empty. It shakes and quivers with exhaustion and I let it fall to the cool grass below.

Pulling myself up, I stand there for a moment, and let my edges gather themselves. For now everything is so quiet. All I hear is my own breath as it whispers in and out of me.

I step back out onto the street and keep moving. The sun is starting to rise above the buildings in the distance and I am thankful for the warmth it will soon bring.

I wonder if my brother will soon come back to try to pick me up. I wonder what I will say when he does.

I have never really ever been good at goodbyes, you know. Nobody ever is. It's just easier to be here one second and gone the next. I think people prefer it that way.

The End

ABOUT THE AUTHOR

Michael James is a writer based in
Saskatoon, Saskatchewan.

Made in the USA
Lexington, KY
22 October 2017